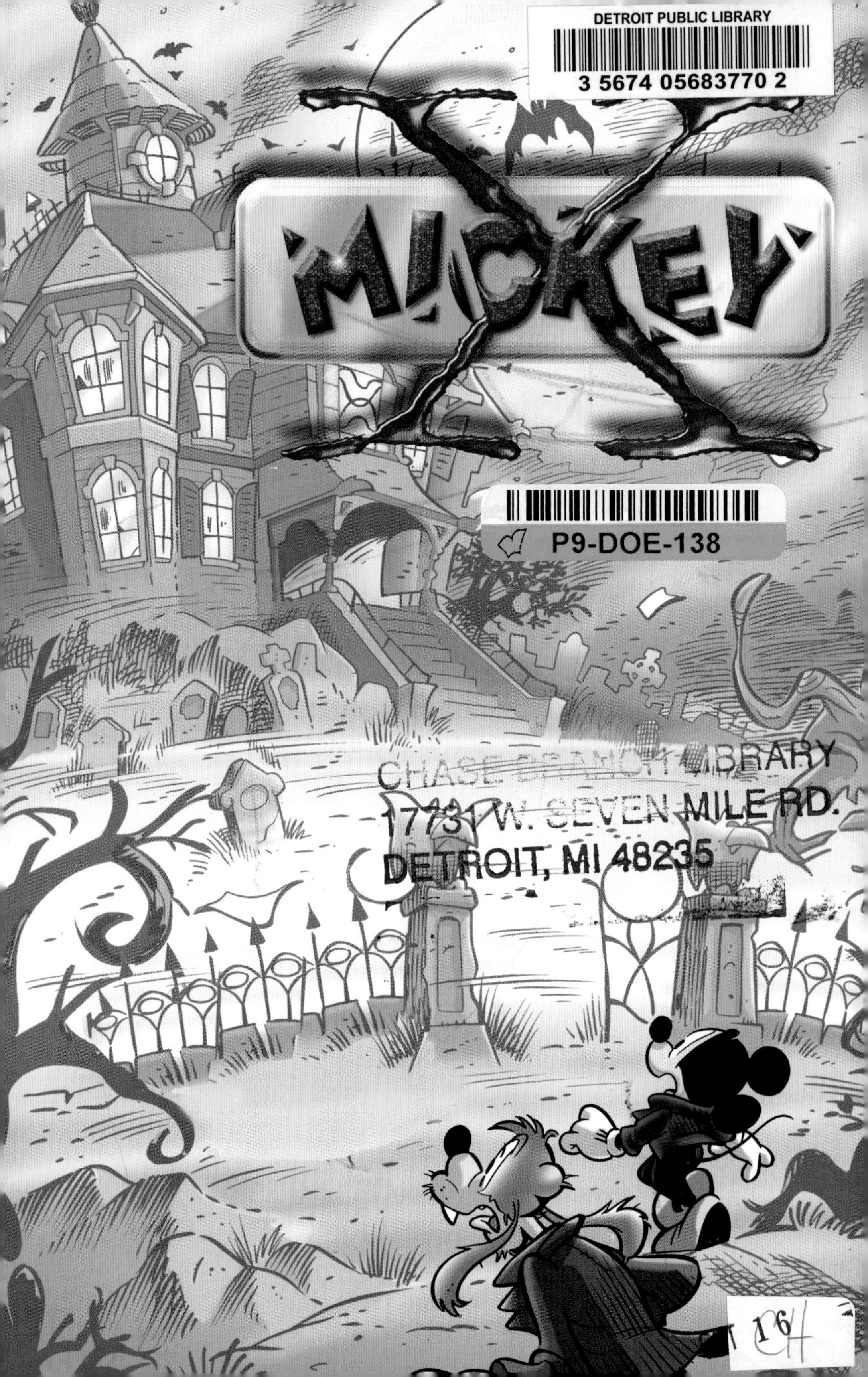
X
MICKEY

Disney FAIRIES

Graphic Novels Available from
PAPERCUTZ

Graphic Novel #1
"Prilla's Talent"

Graphic Novel #2
"Tinker Bell and the
Wings of Rani"

Graphic Novel #3
"Tinker Bell and the
Day of the Dragon"

Graphic Novel #4
"Tinker Bell
to the Rescue"

Graphic Novel #5
"Tinker Bell and the
Pirate Adventure"

Graphic Novel #6
"A Present
for Tinker Bell"

Graphic Novel #7
"Tinker Bell the
Perfect Fairy"

Graphic Novel #8
"Tinker Bell and her
Stories for a Rainy Day"

Graphic Novel #9
"Tinker Bell and
her Magical Arrival"

Graphic Novel #10
"Tinker Bell and
the Lucky Rainbow"

Graphic Novel #11
"Tinker Bell and the
Most Precious Gift"

Graphic Novel #12
"Tinker Bell and the
Lost Treasure"

Graphic Novel #13
"Tinker Bell and the
Pixie Hollow Games"

Graphic Novel #14
"Tinker Bell and
Blaze"

**Tinker Bell
and the Great
Fairy Rescue**

Graphic Novel #15
"Tinker Bell and the
Secret of the Wings"

Graphic Novel #16
"Tinker Bell and the
Pirate Fairy"

Graphic Novel #17
"Tinker Bell and the
Legend of the NeverBeast"

DISNEY FAIRIES graphic novels are available in paperback for $7.99 each;
in hardcover for $12.99 each except #5, $6.99PB, $10.99HC. #6-14 are $7.99PB $11.99HC.
#15 – 18 are $7.99PB $12.99HC.
Tinker Bell and the Great Fairy Rescue is $9.99 in hardcover only.
Available at booksellers everywhere.

See more at papercutz.com

Or you can order from us: Please add $4.00 for postage and handling for first book, and add $1.00 for each additional book.
Please make check payable to NBM Publishing. Send to: Papercutz, 160 Broadway, Suite 700, East Wing, New York, NY 10038
or call 800 886 1223 (9-6 EST M-F) MC-Visa-Amex accepted.

Graphic Novel #18
"Tinker Bell and her
Magical Friends"

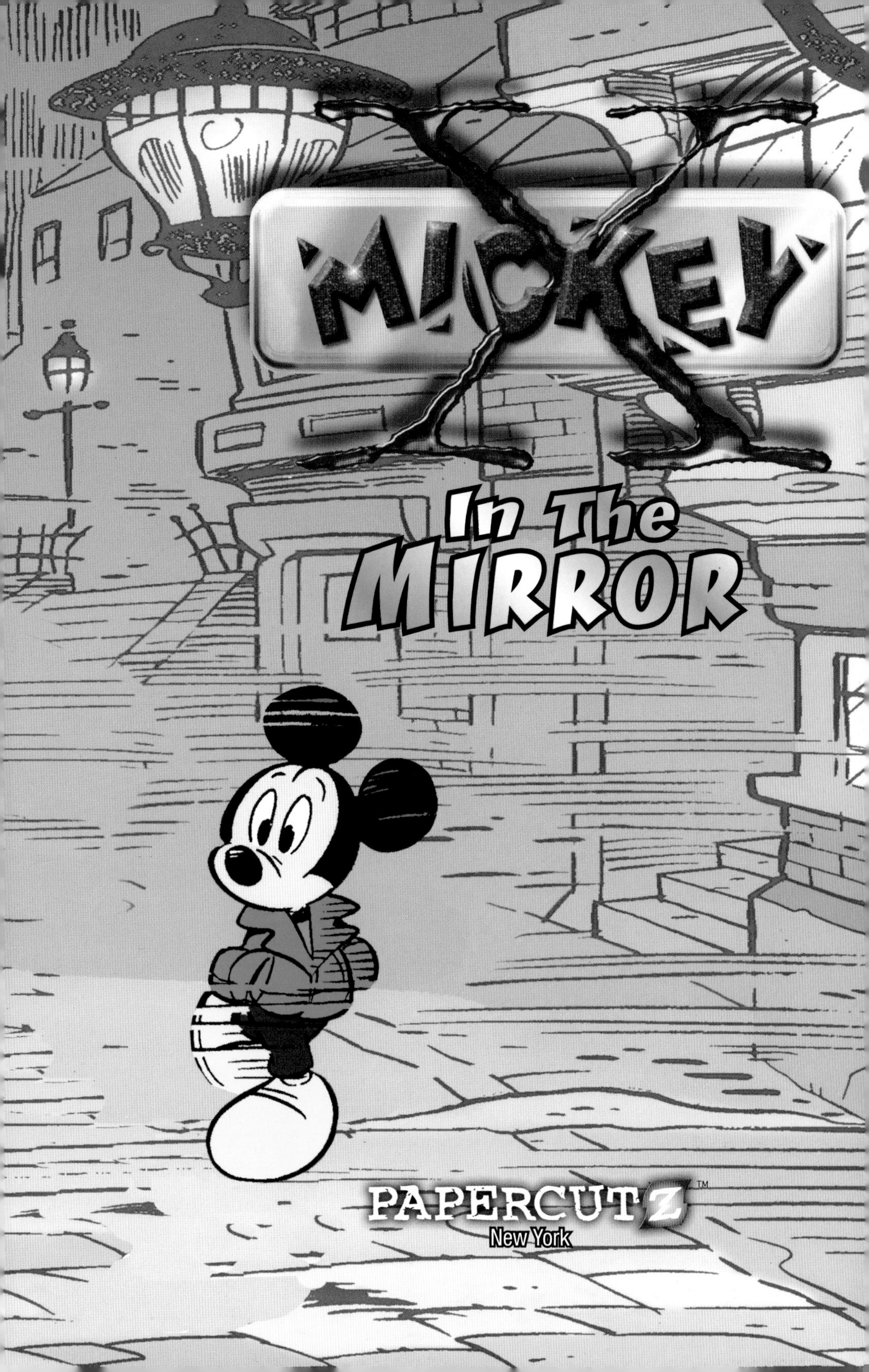
MICKEY X
In The MIRROR
PAPERCUTZ™
New York

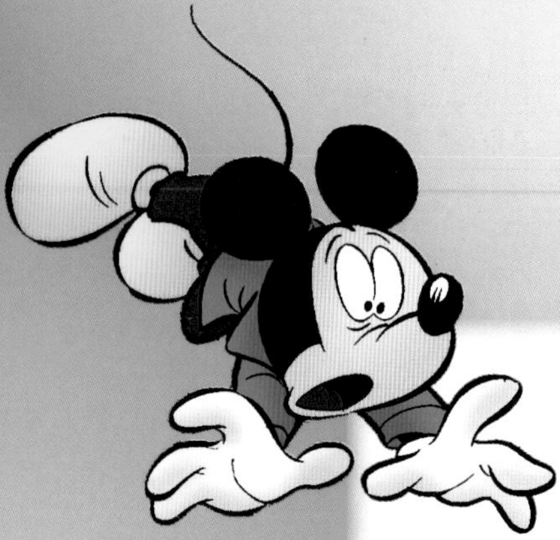

CONTENTS

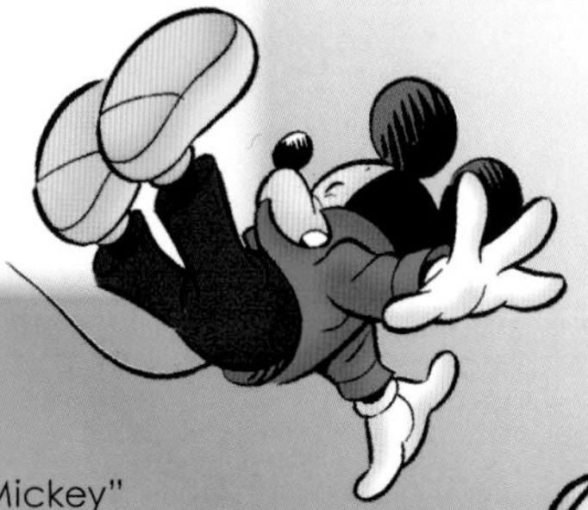

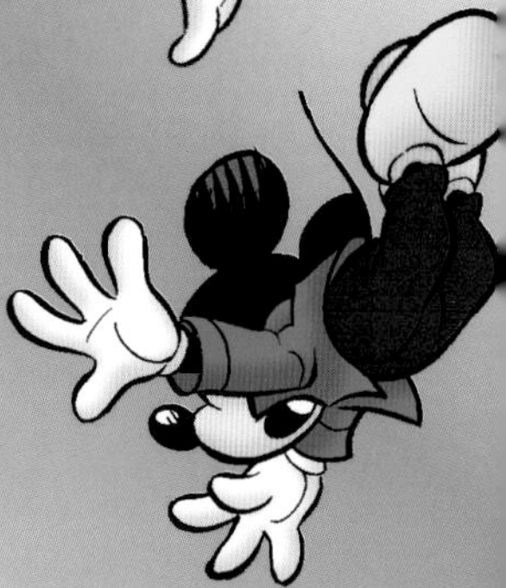

DISNEY GRAPHIC NOVELS #2 "X-Mickey"
"In the Mirror"

Bruno Enna – Writer
Alessandro Perina – Artist
Dawn Guzzo – Production
Jeff Whitman – Production Coordinator
Robert V. Conte – Editor
Bethany Bryan – Associate Editor
Jim Salicrup
Editor-in-Chief

ISBN: 978-162991-4466 Paperback Edition
ISBN: 978-162991-4473 Hardcover Edition

Printed in China through Four Colour Print Group
Printed January 2016 by Samfine Printing (Shenzhen) Co. Ltd
Samfine Industrial Park, Heng Hexing Industrial Zone,
Liaokeng New Villiage Shiyan Town,
Bao'an District Shenzhen, Guandong
China

Papercutz books may be purchased for business or promotional use.
For information on bulk purchases please contact Macmillan Corporate
and Premium Sales Department at
(800) 221-7945 x 5442.

Distributed by Macmillan
First Papercutz Printing

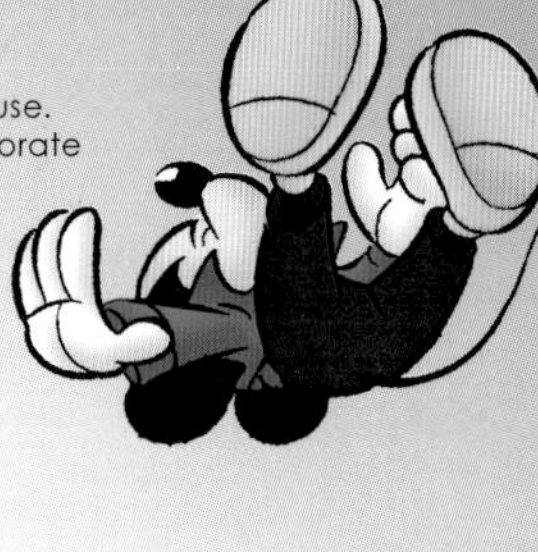

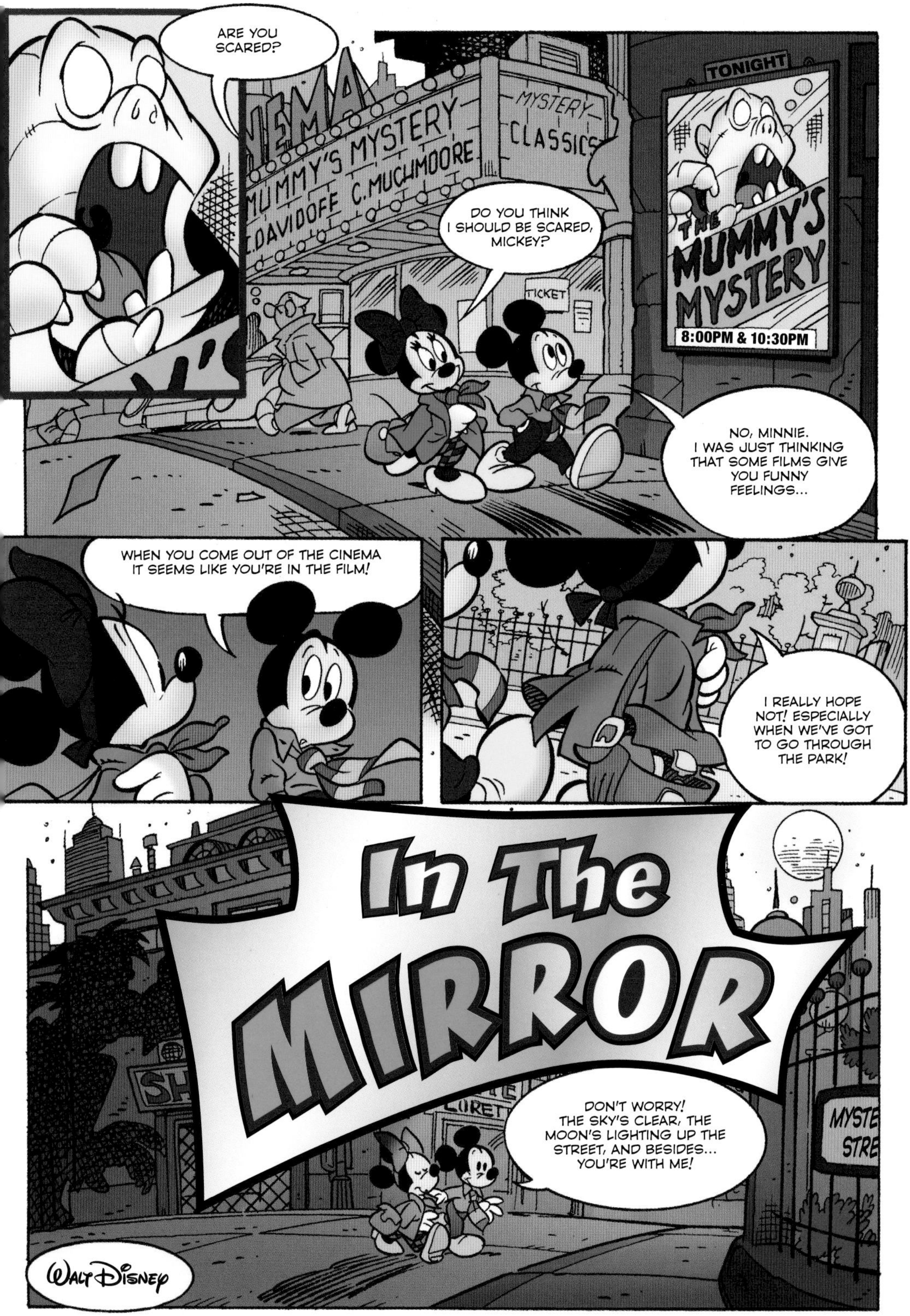
ARE YOU SCARED?
CINEMA
MUMMY'S MYSTERY
C.DAVIDOFF C.MUCHMOORE
MYSTERY CLASSICS
TONIGHT
THE MUMMY'S MYSTERY
8:00PM & 10:30PM
TICKET
DO YOU THINK I SHOULD BE SCARED, MICKEY?
NO, MINNIE. I WAS JUST THINKING THAT SOME FILMS GIVE YOU FUNNY FEELINGS...
WHEN YOU COME OUT OF THE CINEMA IT SEEMS LIKE YOU'RE IN THE FILM!
I REALLY HOPE NOT! ESPECIALLY WHEN WE'VE GOT TO GO THROUGH THE PARK!
In The MIRROR
DON'T WORRY! THE SKY'S CLEAR, THE MOON'S LIGHTING UP THE STREET, AND BESIDES... YOU'RE WITH ME!
WALT DISNEY

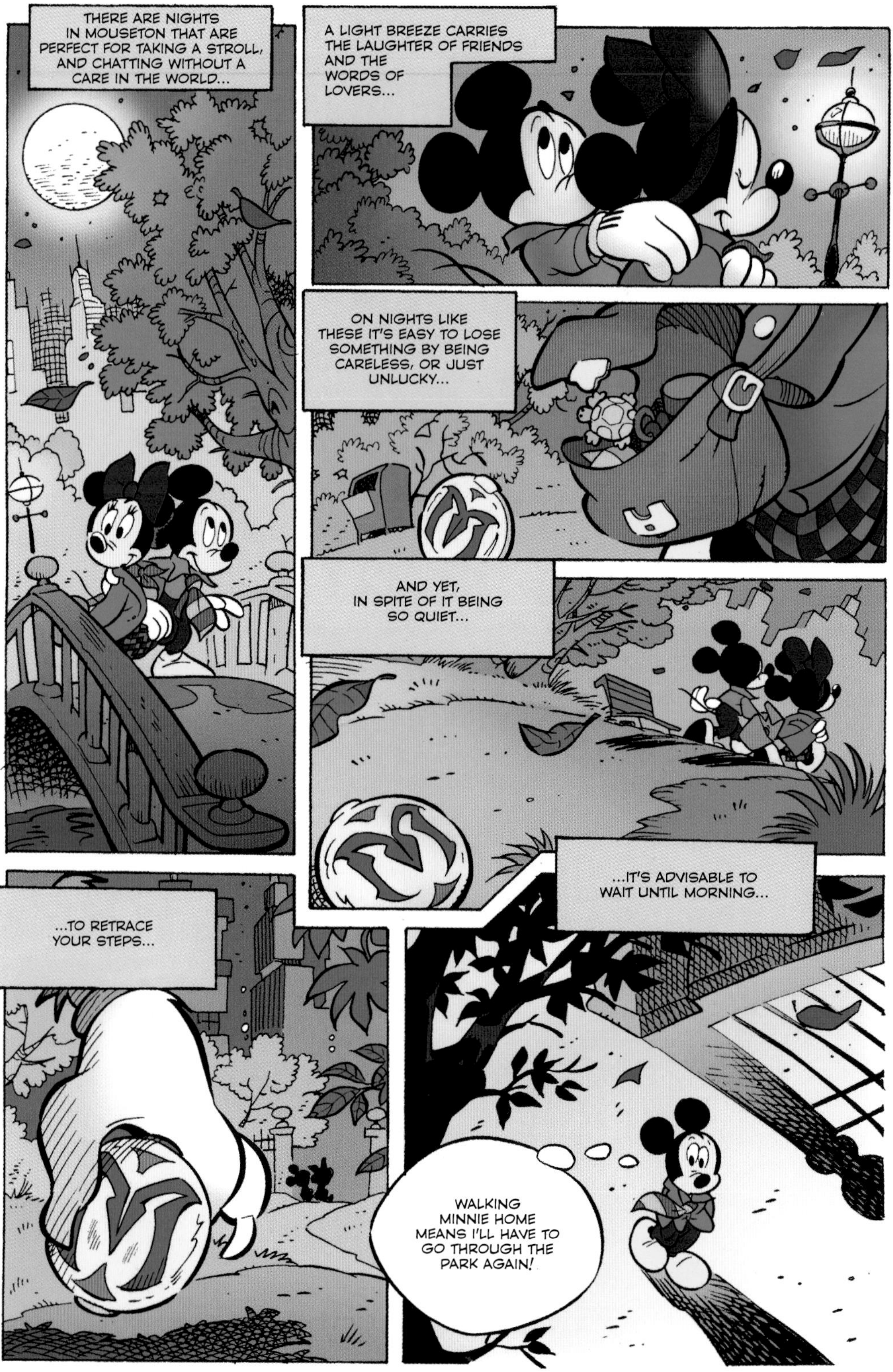
THERE ARE NIGHTS IN MOUSETON THAT ARE PERFECT FOR TAKING A STROLL, AND CHATTING WITHOUT A CARE IN THE WORLD...
A LIGHT BREEZE CARRIES THE LAUGHTER OF FRIENDS AND THE WORDS OF LOVERS...
ON NIGHTS LIKE THESE IT'S EASY TO LOSE SOMETHING BY BEING CARELESS, OR JUST UNLUCKY...
AND YET, IN SPITE OF IT BEING SO QUIET...
...IT'S ADVISABLE TO WAIT UNTIL MORNING...
...TO RETRACE YOUR STEPS...
WALKING MINNIE HOME MEANS I'LL HAVE TO GO THROUGH THE PARK AGAIN!

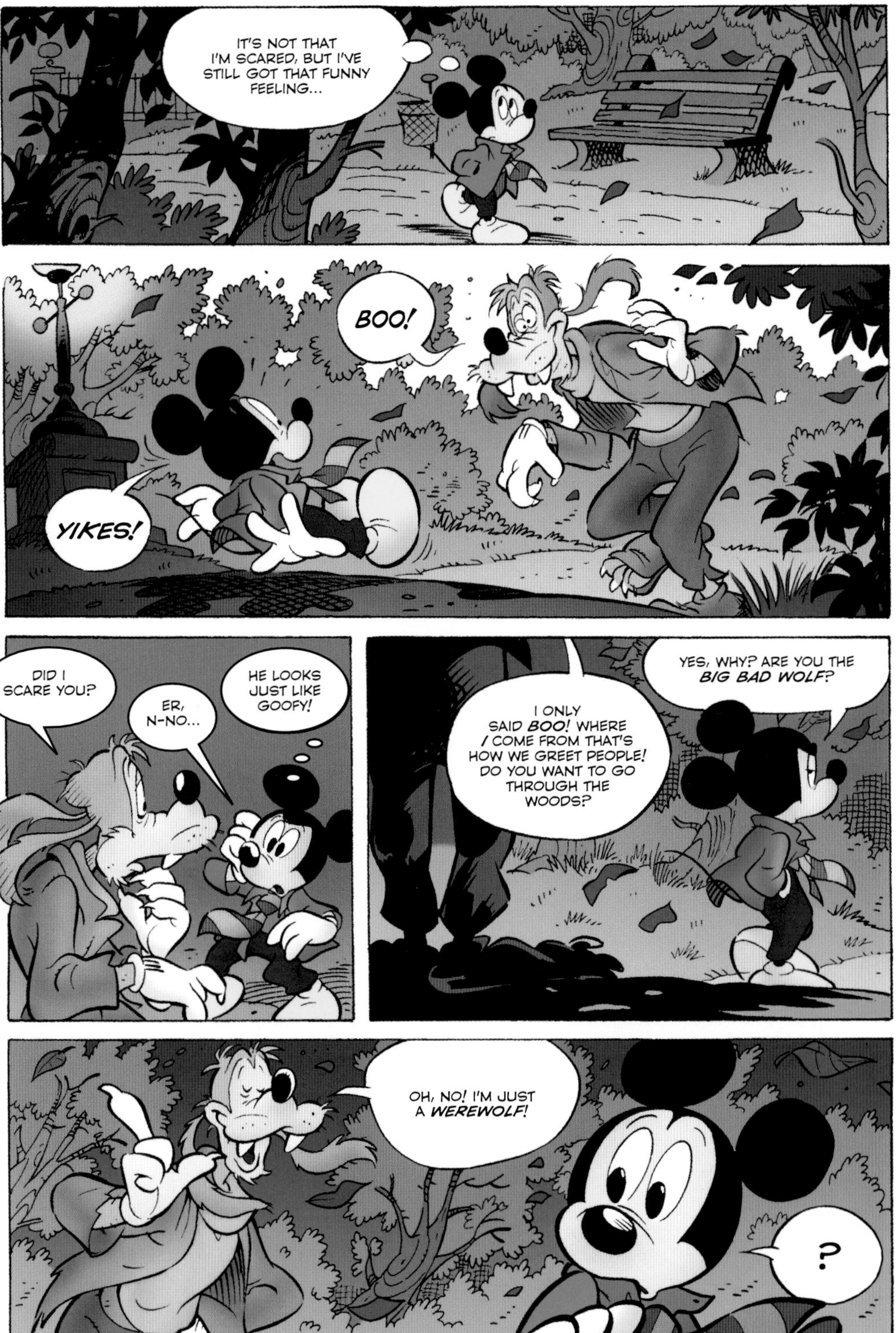
IT'S NOT THAT I'M SCARED, BUT I'VE STILL GOT THAT FUNNY FEELING...
BOO!
YIKES!
DID I SCARE YOU?
ER, N-NO...
HE LOOKS JUST LIKE GOOFY!
YES, WHY? ARE YOU THE BIG BAD WOLF?
I ONLY SAID BOO! WHERE I COME FROM THAT'S HOW WE GREET PEOPLE! DO YOU WANT TO GO THROUGH THE WOODS?
OH, NO! I'M JUST A WEREWOLF!
?

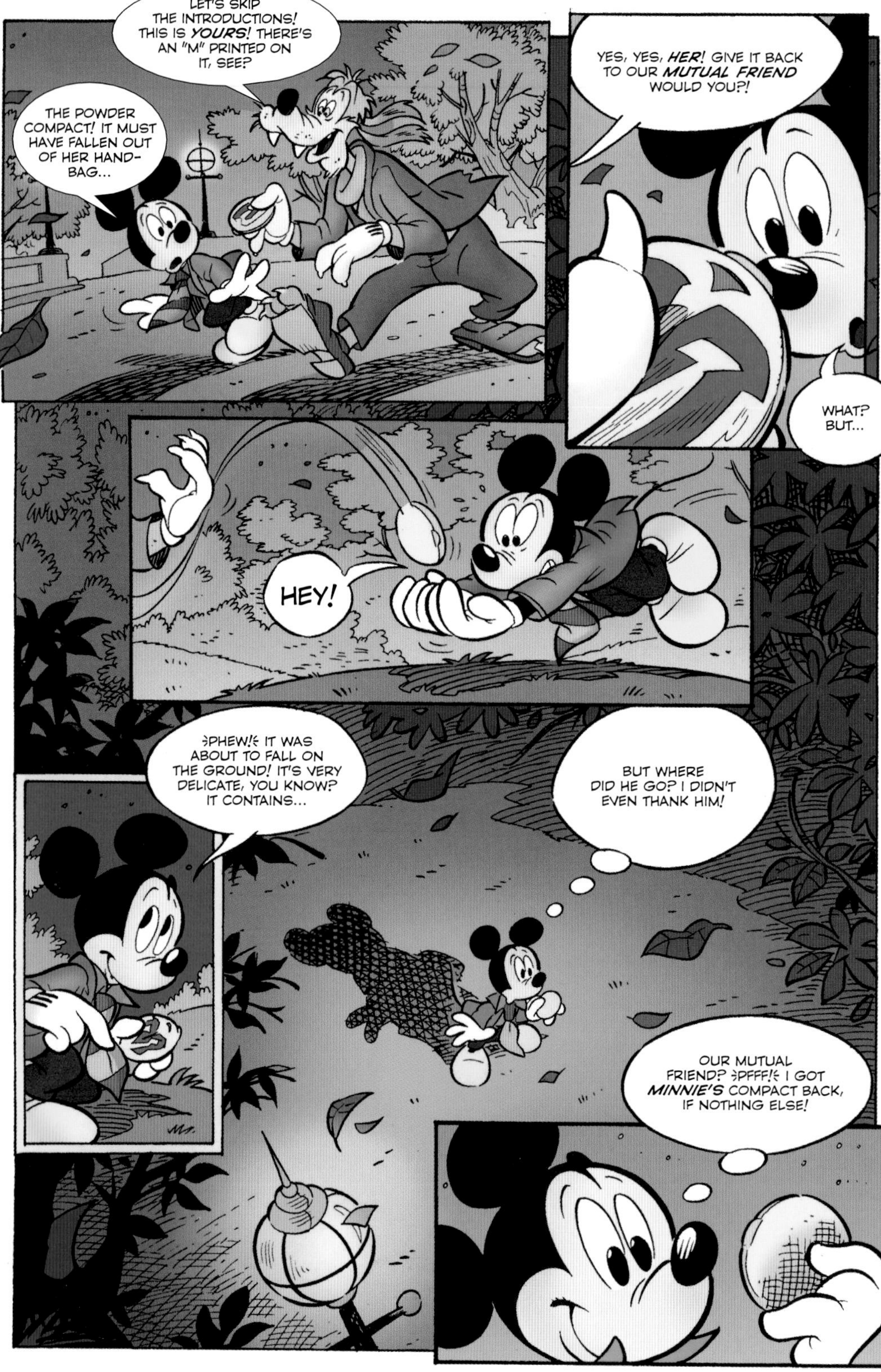
THE POWDER COMPACT! IT MUST HAVE FALLEN OUT OF HER HAND-BAG...
LET'S SKIP THE INTRODUCTIONS! THIS IS YOURS! THERE'S AN "M" PRINTED ON IT, SEE?
YES, YES, HER! GIVE IT BACK TO OUR MUTUAL FRIEND WOULD YOU?!
WHAT? BUT...
HEY!
¦PHEW!¦ IT WAS ABOUT TO FALL ON THE GROUND! IT'S VERY DELICATE, YOU KNOW? IT CONTAINS...
BUT WHERE DID HE GO? I DIDN'T EVEN THANK HIM!
OUR MUTUAL FRIEND? ¦PFFF!¦ I GOT MINNIE'S COMPACT BACK, IF NOTHING ELSE!

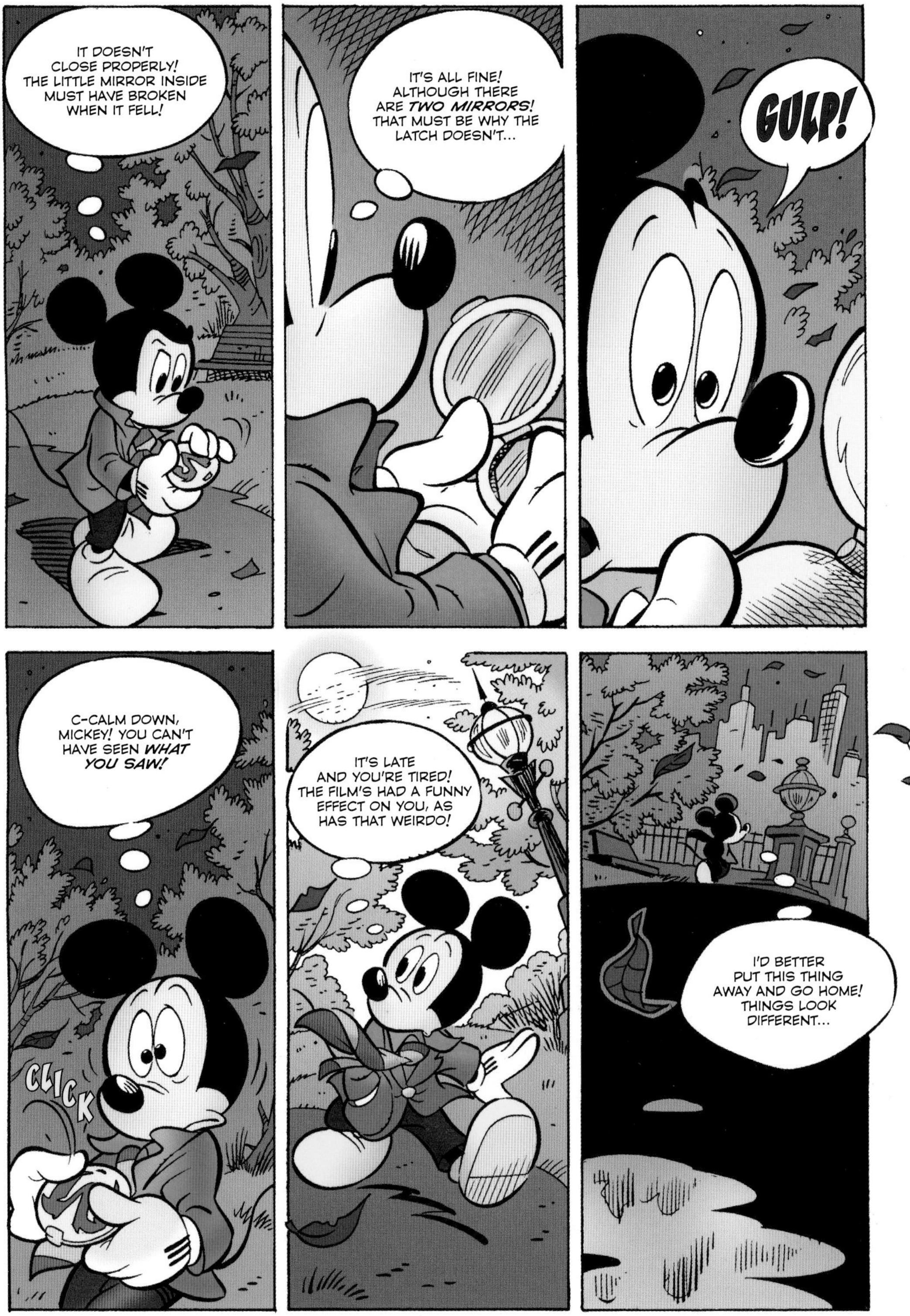
IT DOESN'T CLOSE PROPERLY! THE LITTLE MIRROR INSIDE MUST HAVE BROKEN WHEN IT FELL!
IT'S ALL FINE! ALTHOUGH THERE ARE *TWO MIRRORS!* THAT MUST BE WHY THE LATCH DOESN'T...
GULP!
C-CALM DOWN, MICKEY! YOU CAN'T HAVE SEEN *WHAT YOU SAW!*
CLICK
IT'S LATE AND YOU'RE TIRED! THE FILM'S HAD A FUNNY EFFECT ON YOU, AS HAS THAT WEIRDO!
I'D BETTER PUT THIS THING AWAY AND GO HOME! THINGS LOOK DIFFERENT...

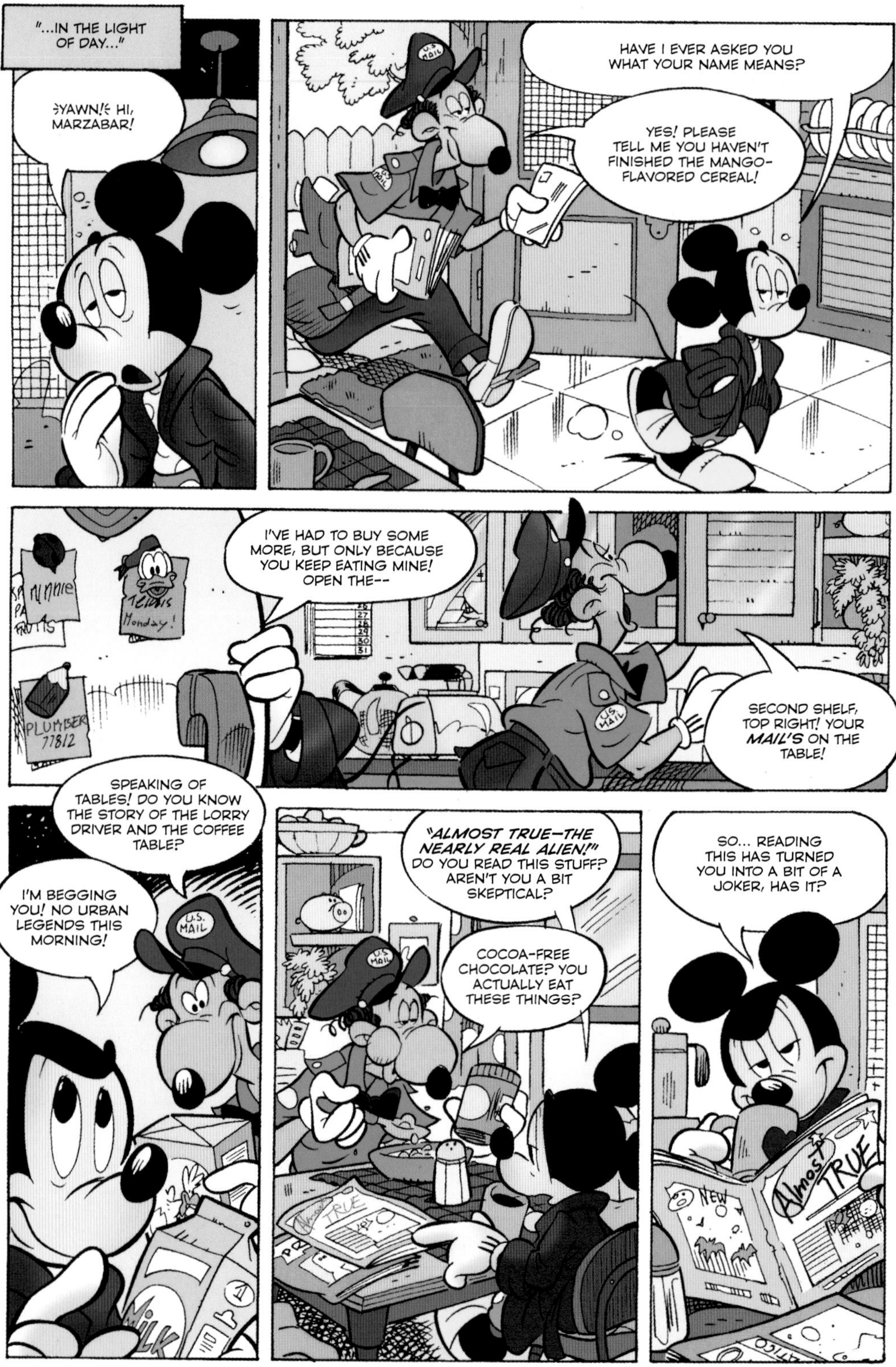

"...IN THE LIGHT OF DAY..."
≶YAWN!≶ HI, MARZABAR!
HAVE I EVER ASKED YOU WHAT YOUR NAME MEANS?
YES! PLEASE TELL ME YOU HAVEN'T FINISHED THE MANGO-FLAVORED CEREAL!
I'VE HAD TO BUY SOME MORE, BUT ONLY BECAUSE YOU KEEP EATING MINE! OPEN THE--
SECOND SHELF, TOP RIGHT! YOUR MAIL'S ON THE TABLE!
PLUMBER 77812
SPEAKING OF TABLES! DO YOU KNOW THE STORY OF THE LORRY DRIVER AND THE COFFEE TABLE?
I'M BEGGING YOU! NO URBAN LEGENDS THIS MORNING!
"ALMOST TRUE—THE NEARLY REAL ALIEN!" DO YOU READ THIS STUFF? AREN'T YOU A BIT SKEPTICAL?
COCOA-FREE CHOCOLATE? YOU ACTUALLY EAT THESE THINGS?
SO... READING THIS HAS TURNED YOU INTO A BIT OF A JOKER, HAS IT?

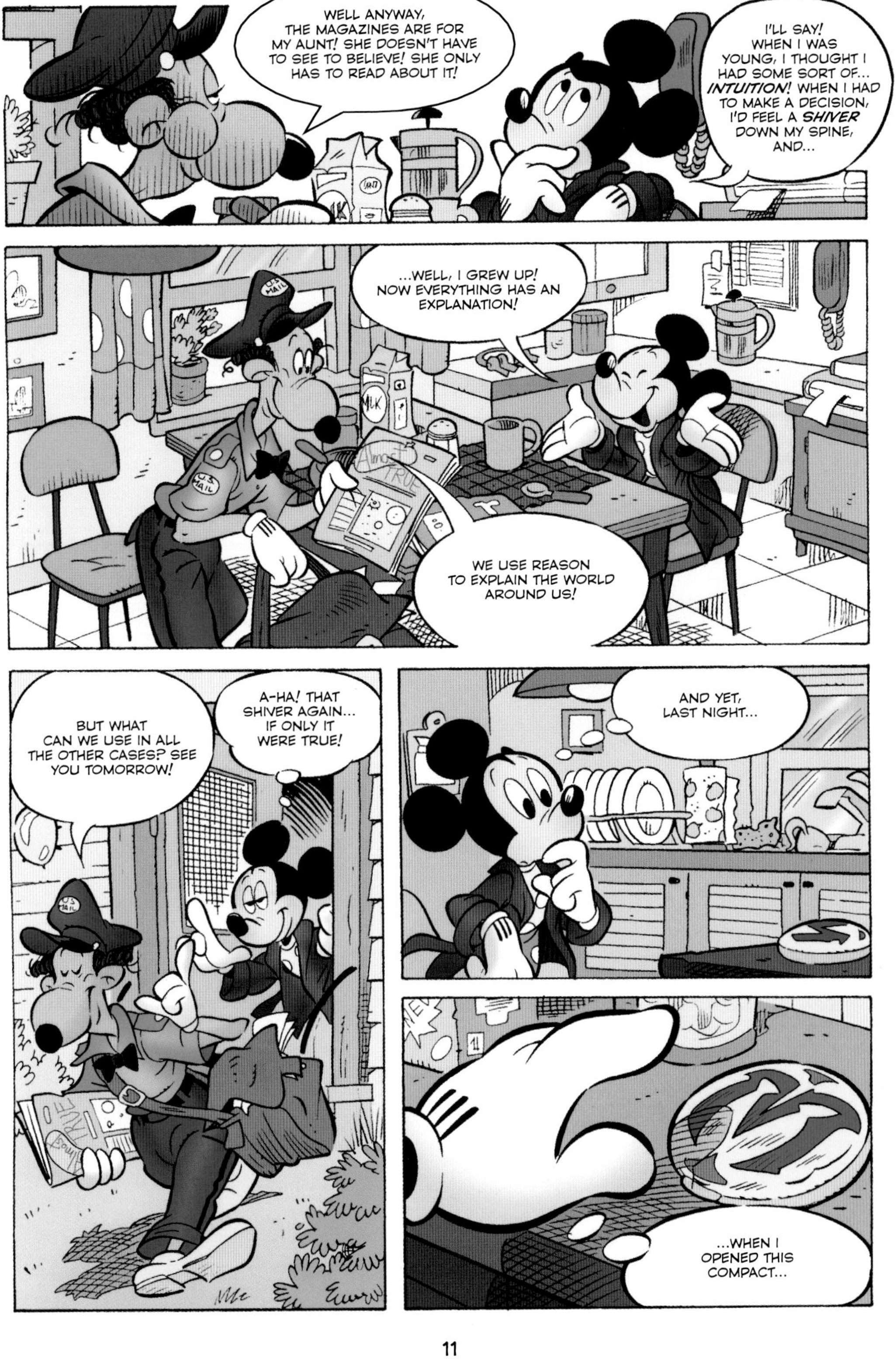
WELL ANYWAY, THE MAGAZINES ARE FOR MY AUNT! SHE DOESN'T HAVE TO SEE TO BELIEVE! SHE ONLY HAS TO READ ABOUT IT!
I'LL SAY! WHEN I WAS YOUNG, I THOUGHT I HAD SOME SORT OF... INTUITION! WHEN I HAD TO MAKE A DECISION, I'D FEEL A SHIVER DOWN MY SPINE, AND...
...WELL, I GREW UP! NOW EVERYTHING HAS AN EXPLANATION!
WE USE REASON TO EXPLAIN THE WORLD AROUND US!
BUT WHAT CAN WE USE IN ALL THE OTHER CASES? SEE YOU TOMORROW!
A-HA! THAT SHIVER AGAIN... IF ONLY IT WERE TRUE!
AND YET, LAST NIGHT...
...WHEN I OPENED THIS COMPACT...

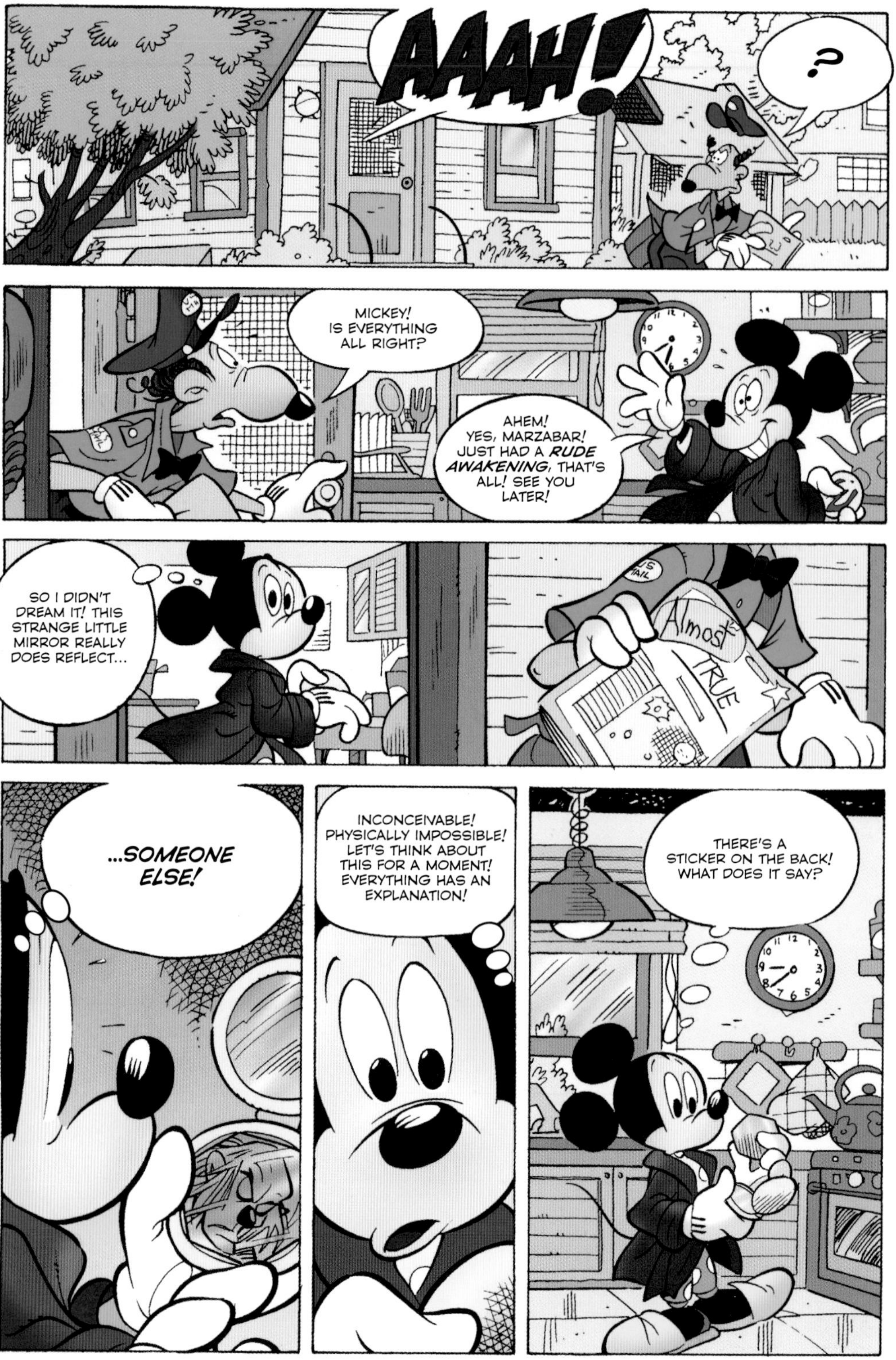
AAAH!
?
MICKEY! IS EVERYTHING ALL RIGHT?
AHEM! YES, MARZABAR! JUST HAD A RUDE AWAKENING, THAT'S ALL! SEE YOU LATER!
SO I DIDN'T DREAM IT! THIS STRANGE LITTLE MIRROR REALLY DOES REFLECT...
Almost TRUE
...SOMEONE ELSE!
INCONCEIVABLE! PHYSICALLY IMPOSSIBLE! LET'S THINK ABOUT THIS FOR A MOMENT! EVERYTHING HAS AN EXPLANATION!
THERE'S A STICKER ON THE BACK! WHAT DOES IT SAY?

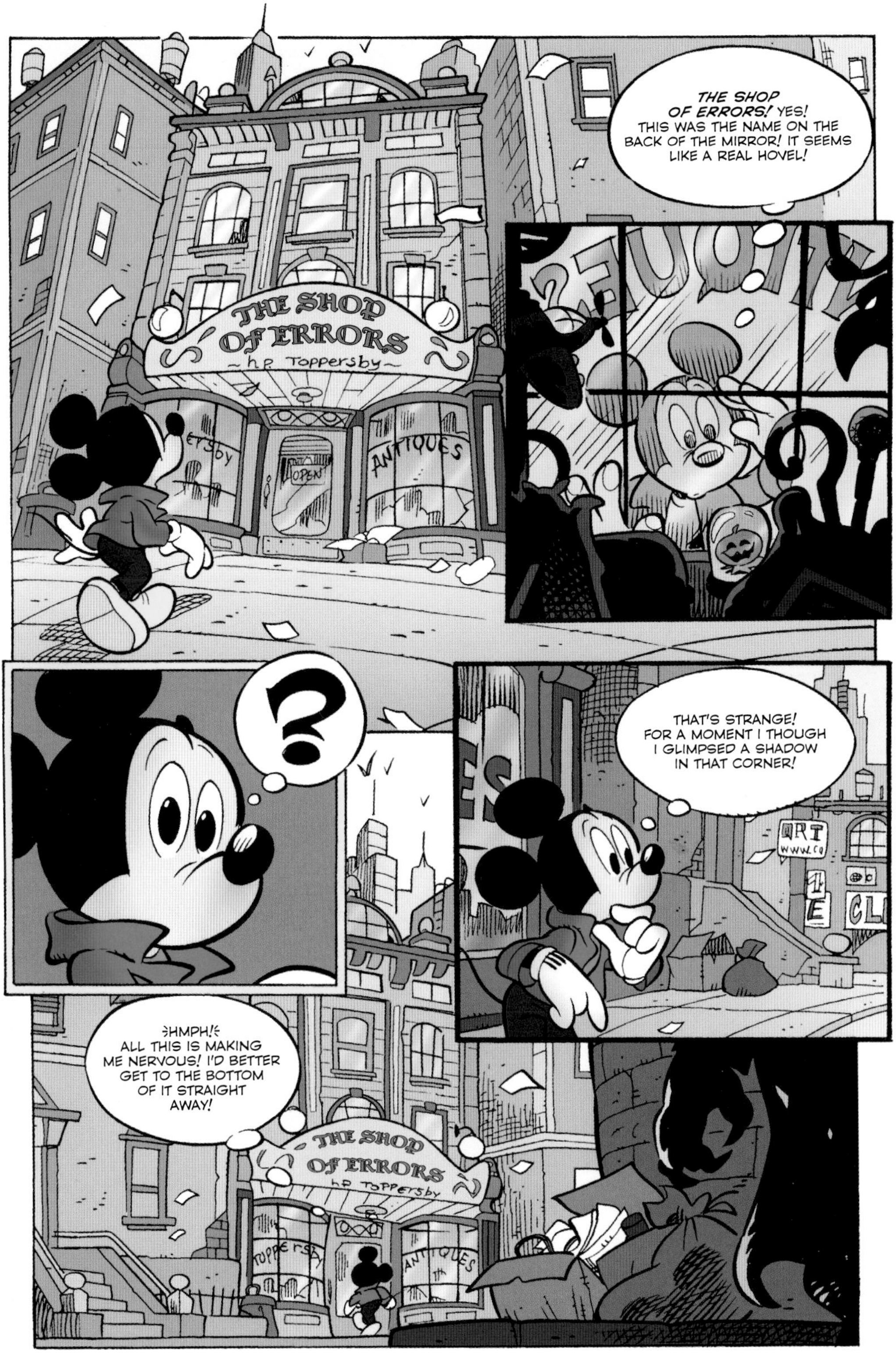
THE SHOP OF ERRORS! YES! THIS WAS THE NAME ON THE BACK OF THE MIRROR! IT SEEMS LIKE A REAL HOVEL!
THE SHOP OF ERRORS
h.p. Toppersby
ANTIQUES
OPEN
?
THAT'S STRANGE! FOR A MOMENT I THOUGH I GLIMPSED A SHADOW IN THAT CORNER!
HMPH! ALL THIS IS MAKING ME NERVOUS! I'D BETTER GET TO THE BOTTOM OF IT STRAIGHT AWAY!
THE SHOP OF ERRORS
h.p. Toppersby
ANTIQUES

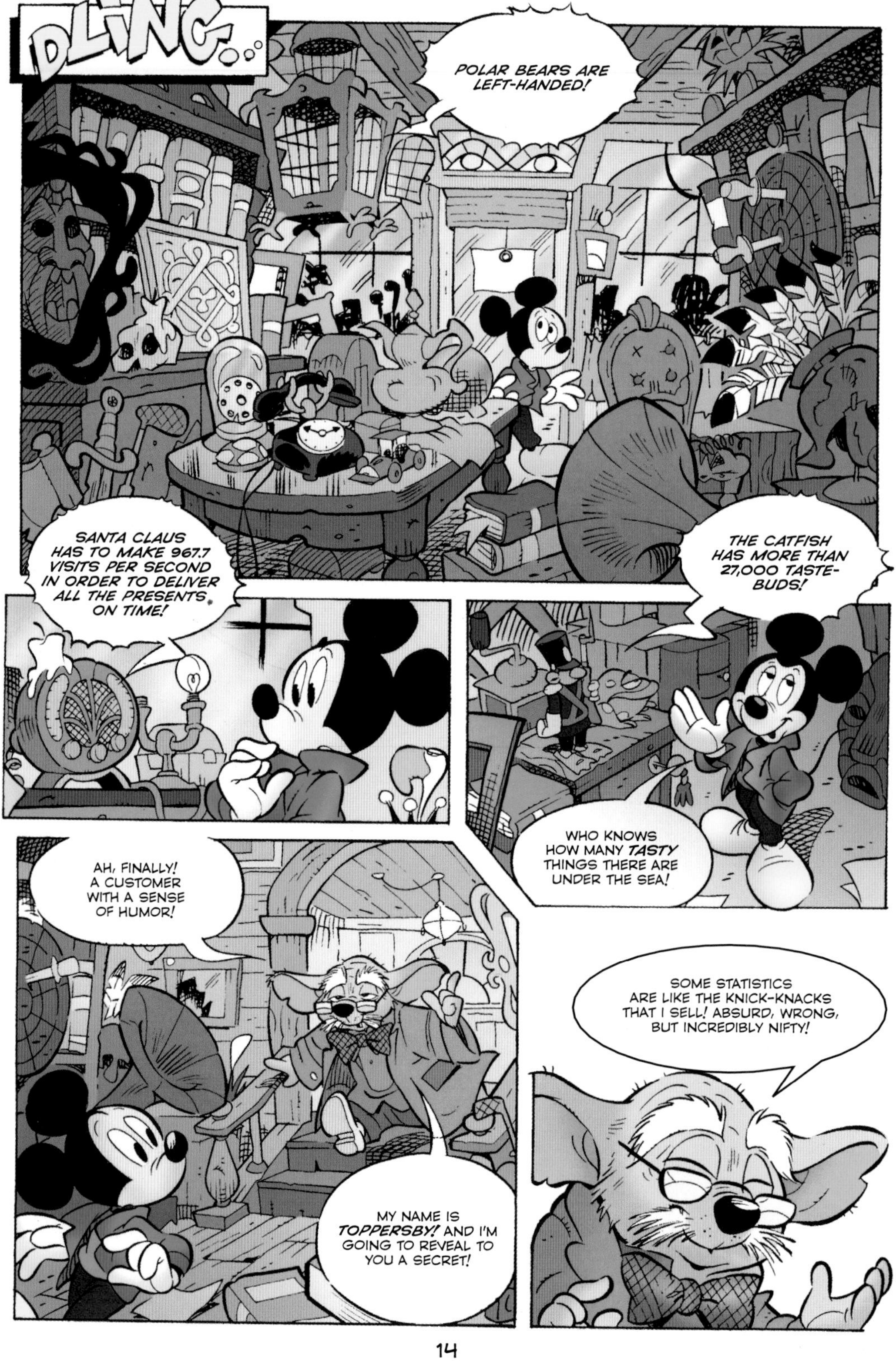
DLING...
POLAR BEARS ARE LEFT-HANDED!
SANTA CLAUS HAS TO MAKE 967.7 VISITS PER SECOND IN ORDER TO DELIVER ALL THE PRESENTS ON TIME!
THE CATFISH HAS MORE THAN 27,000 TASTE-BUDS!
WHO KNOWS HOW MANY TASTY THINGS THERE ARE UNDER THE SEA!
AH, FINALLY! A CUSTOMER WITH A SENSE OF HUMOR!
MY NAME IS TOPPERSBY! AND I'M GOING TO REVEAL TO YOU A SECRET!
SOME STATISTICS ARE LIKE THE KNICK-KNACKS THAT I SELL! ABSURD, WRONG, BUT INCREDIBLY NIFTY!

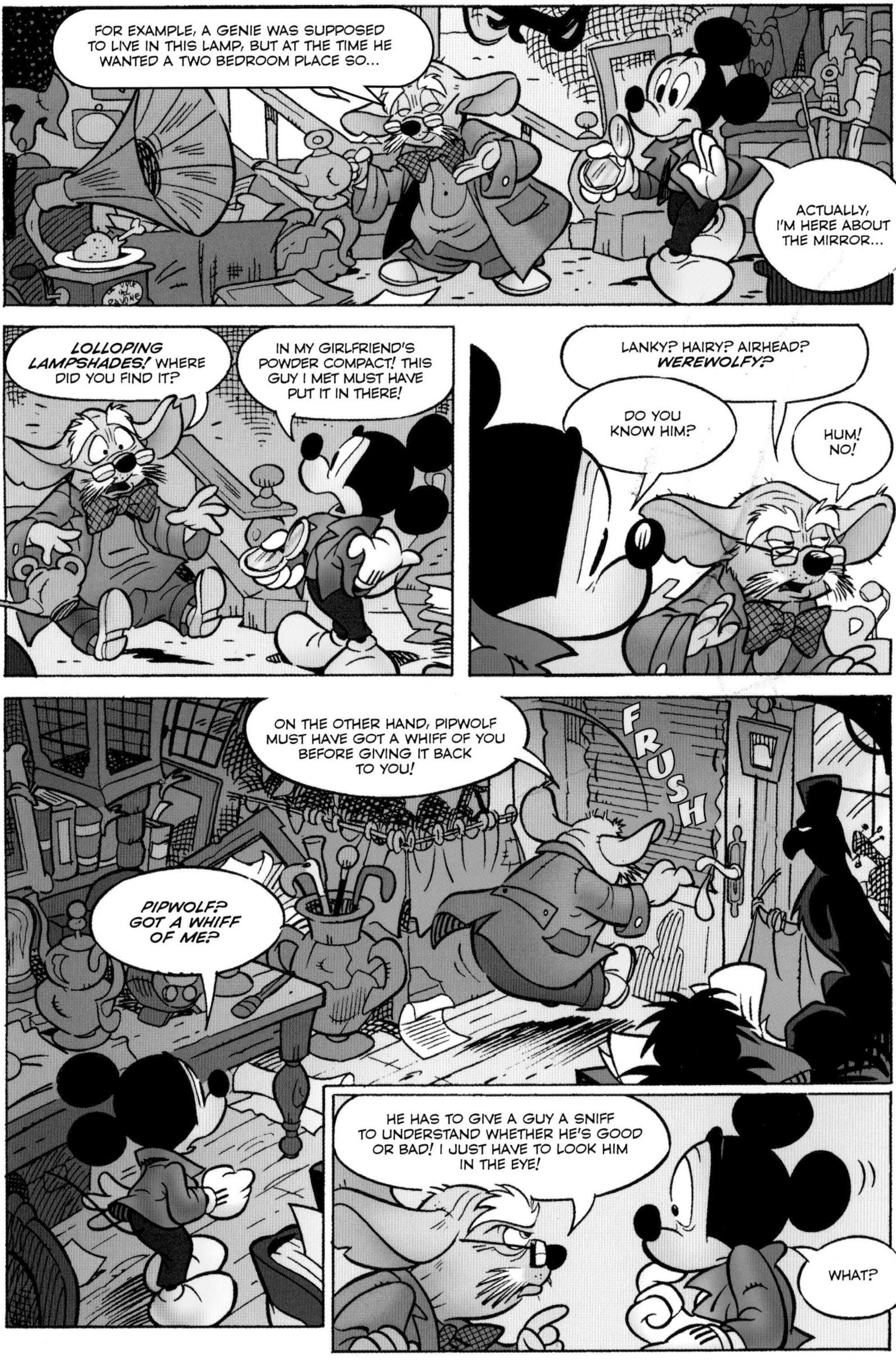
FOR EXAMPLE, A GENIE WAS SUPPOSED TO LIVE IN THIS LAMP, BUT AT THE TIME HE WANTED A TWO BEDROOM PLACE SO...
ACTUALLY, I'M HERE ABOUT THE MIRROR...
LOLLOPING LAMPSHADES! WHERE DID YOU FIND IT?
IN MY GIRLFRIEND'S POWDER COMPACT! THIS GUY I MET MUST HAVE PUT IT IN THERE!
LANKY? HAIRY? AIRHEAD? WEREWOLFY?
DO YOU KNOW HIM?
HUM! NO!
ON THE OTHER HAND, PIPWOLF MUST HAVE GOT A WHIFF OF YOU BEFORE GIVING IT BACK TO YOU!
FRUSH
PIPWOLF? GOT A WHIFF OF ME?
HE HAS TO GIVE A GUY A SNIFF TO UNDERSTAND WHETHER HE'S GOOD OR BAD! I JUST HAVE TO LOOK HIM IN THE EYE!
WHAT?

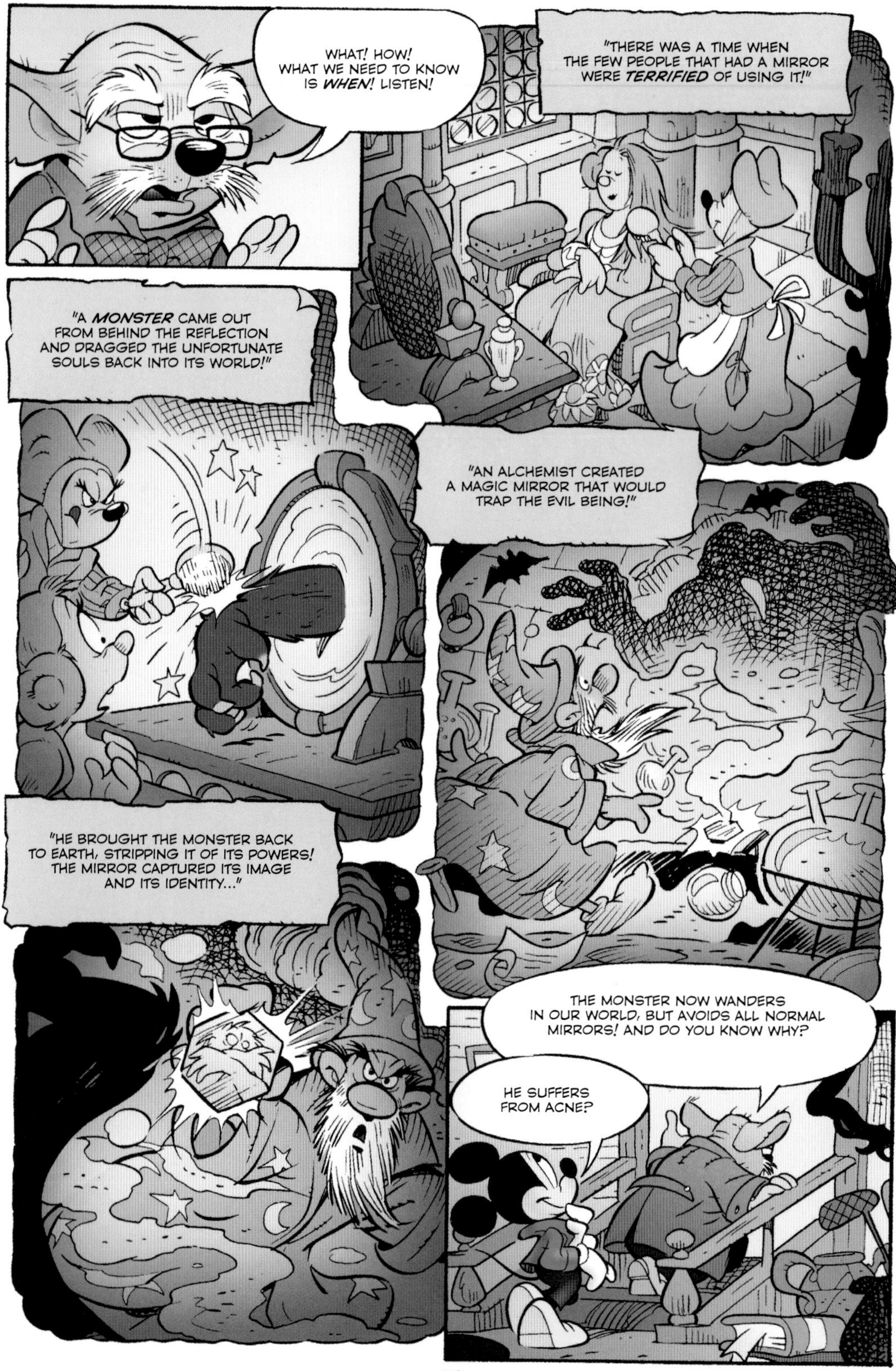
WHAT! HOW! WHAT WE NEED TO KNOW IS WHEN! LISTEN!
"THERE WAS A TIME WHEN THE FEW PEOPLE THAT HAD A MIRROR WERE TERRIFIED OF USING IT!"
"A MONSTER CAME OUT FROM BEHIND THE REFLECTION AND DRAGGED THE UNFORTUNATE SOULS BACK INTO ITS WORLD!"
"AN ALCHEMIST CREATED A MAGIC MIRROR THAT WOULD TRAP THE EVIL BEING!"
"HE BROUGHT THE MONSTER BACK TO EARTH, STRIPPING IT OF ITS POWERS! THE MIRROR CAPTURED ITS IMAGE AND ITS IDENTITY..."
THE MONSTER NOW WANDERS IN OUR WORLD, BUT AVOIDS ALL NORMAL MIRRORS! AND DO YOU KNOW WHY?
HE SUFFERS FROM ACNE?

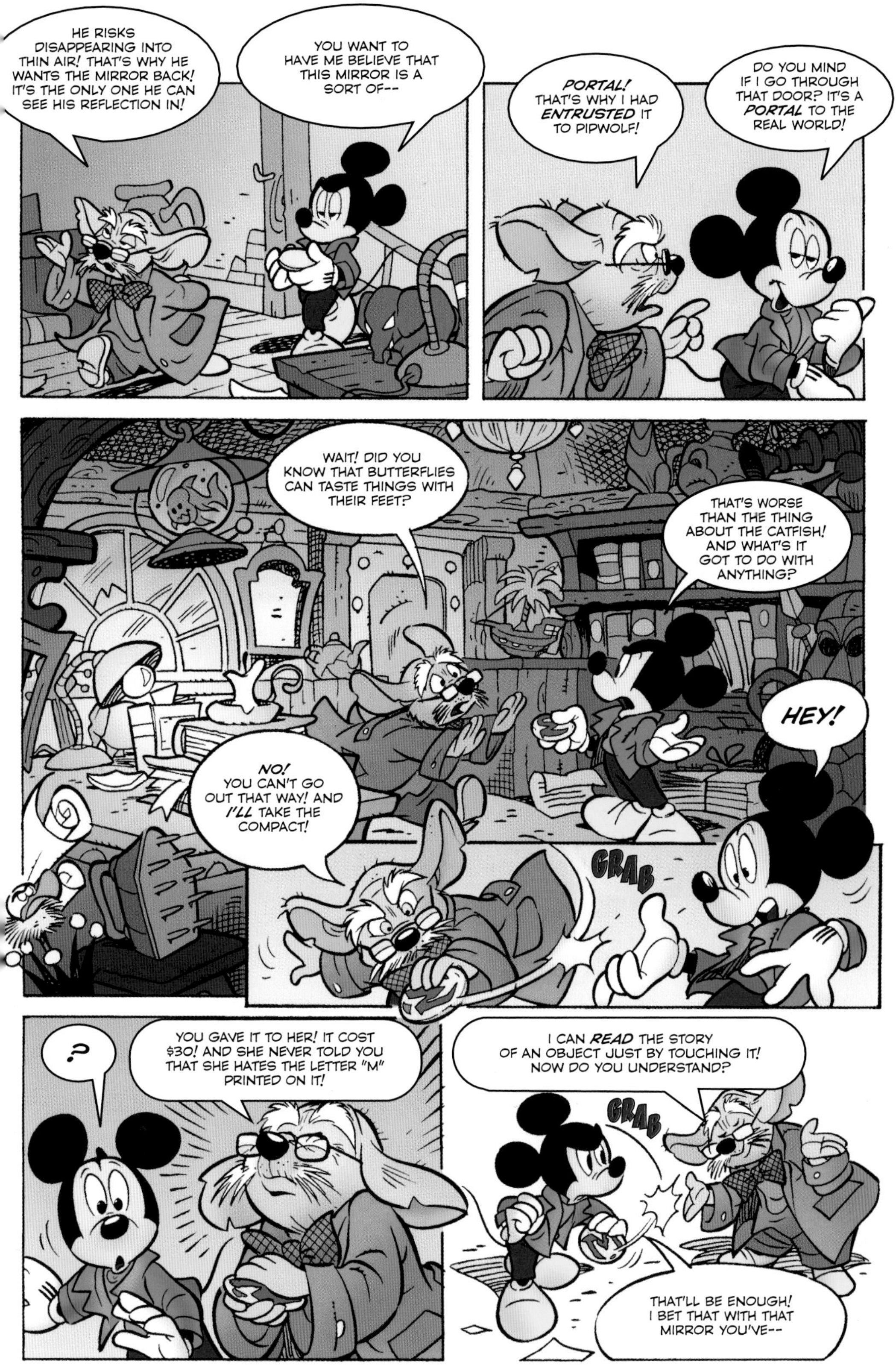
HE RISKS DISAPPEARING INTO THIN AIR! THAT'S WHY HE WANTS THE MIRROR BACK! IT'S THE ONLY ONE HE CAN SEE HIS REFLECTION IN!
YOU WANT TO HAVE ME BELIEVE THAT THIS MIRROR IS A SORT OF--
PORTAL! THAT'S WHY I HAD ENTRUSTED IT TO PIPWOLF!
DO YOU MIND IF I GO THROUGH THAT DOOR? IT'S A PORTAL TO THE REAL WORLD!
WAIT! DID YOU KNOW THAT BUTTERFLIES CAN TASTE THINGS WITH THEIR FEET?
THAT'S WORSE THAN THE THING ABOUT THE CATFISH! AND WHAT'S IT GOT TO DO WITH ANYTHING?
NO! YOU CAN'T GO OUT THAT WAY! AND I'LL TAKE THE COMPACT!
HEY!
GRAB
?
YOU GAVE IT TO HER! IT COST $30! AND SHE NEVER TOLD YOU THAT SHE HATES THE LETTER "M" PRINTED ON IT!
I CAN READ THE STORY OF AN OBJECT JUST BY TOUCHING IT! NOW DO YOU UNDERSTAND?
GRAB
THAT'LL BE ENOUGH! I BET THAT WITH THAT MIRROR YOU'VE--

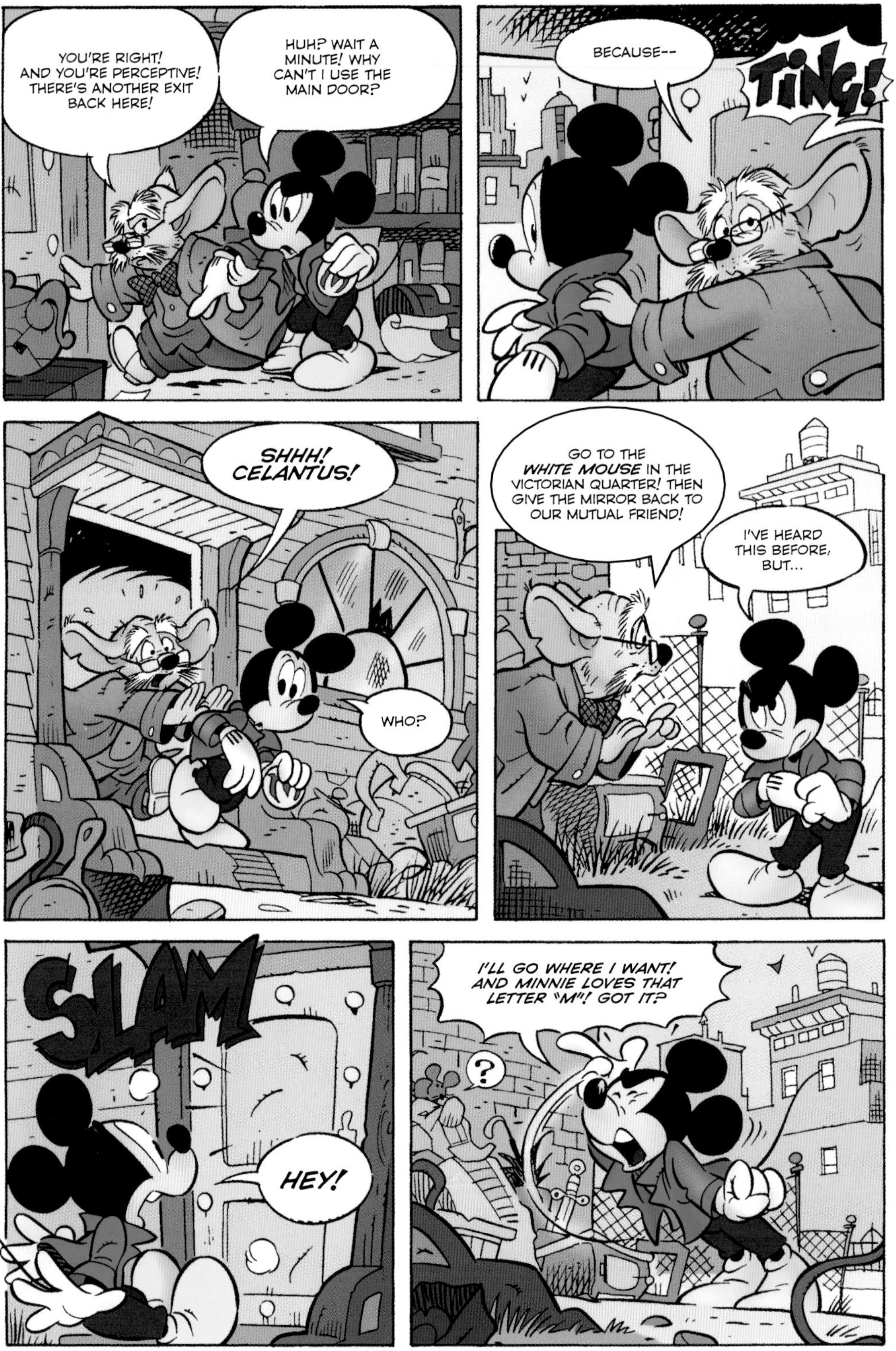
YOU'RE RIGHT! AND YOU'RE PERCEPTIVE! THERE'S ANOTHER EXIT BACK HERE!
HUH? WAIT A MINUTE! WHY CAN'T I USE THE MAIN DOOR?
BECAUSE--
TING!
SHHH! CELANTUS!
WHO?
GO TO THE WHITE MOUSE IN THE VICTORIAN QUARTER! THEN GIVE THE MIRROR BACK TO OUR MUTUAL FRIEND!
I'VE HEARD THIS BEFORE, BUT...
SLAM
HEY!
I'LL GO WHERE I WANT! AND MINNIE LOVES THAT LETTER "M"! GOT IT?
?

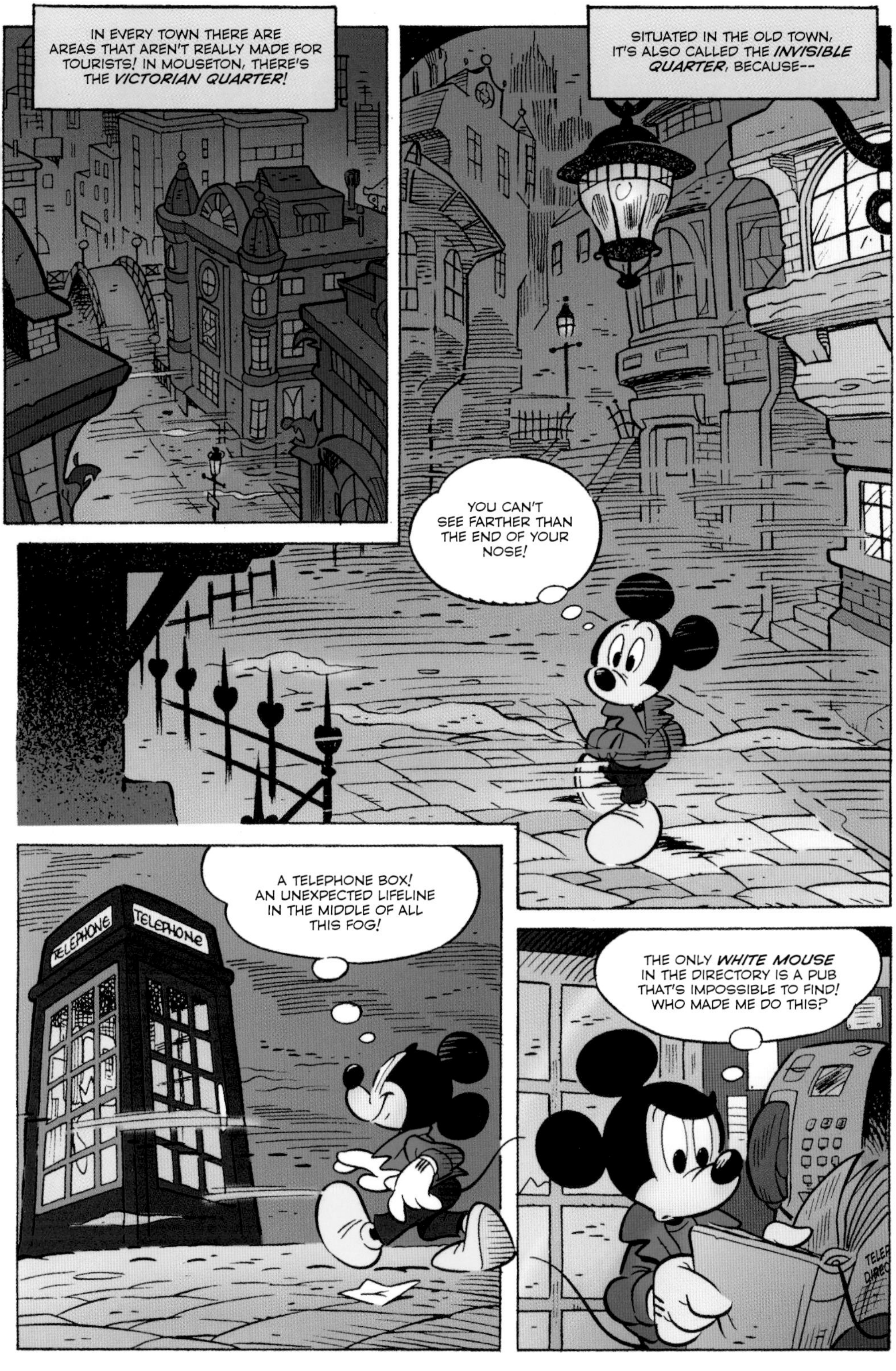
IN EVERY TOWN THERE ARE AREAS THAT AREN'T REALLY MADE FOR TOURISTS! IN MOUSETON, THERE'S THE *VICTORIAN QUARTER!*
SITUATED IN THE OLD TOWN, IT'S ALSO CALLED THE *INVISIBLE QUARTER*, BECAUSE--
YOU CAN'T SEE FARTHER THAN THE END OF YOUR NOSE!
A TELEPHONE BOX! AN UNEXPECTED LIFELINE IN THE MIDDLE OF ALL THIS FOG!
TELEPHONE
TELEPHONE
THE ONLY ***WHITE MOUSE*** IN THE DIRECTORY IS A PUB THAT'S IMPOSSIBLE TO FIND! WHO MADE ME DO THIS?

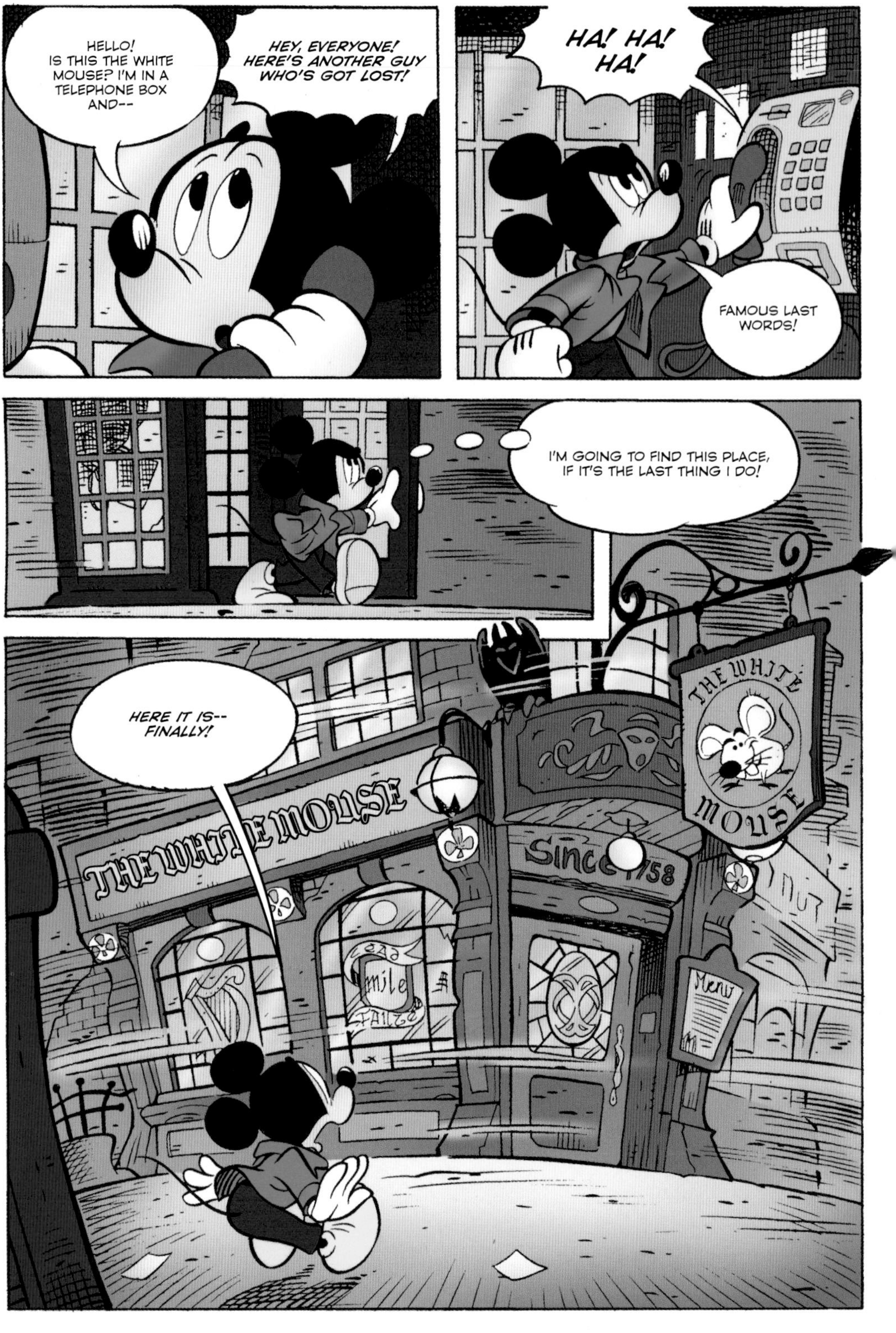

HELLO! IS THIS THE WHITE MOUSE? I'M IN A TELEPHONE BOX AND--
HEY, EVERYONE! HERE'S ANOTHER GUY WHO'S GOT LOST!
HA! HA! HA!
FAMOUS LAST WORDS!
I'M GOING TO FIND THIS PLACE, IF IT'S THE LAST THING I DO!
HERE IT IS-- FINALLY!
THE WHITE MOUSE
THE WHITE MOUSE
Since 1758
Menu

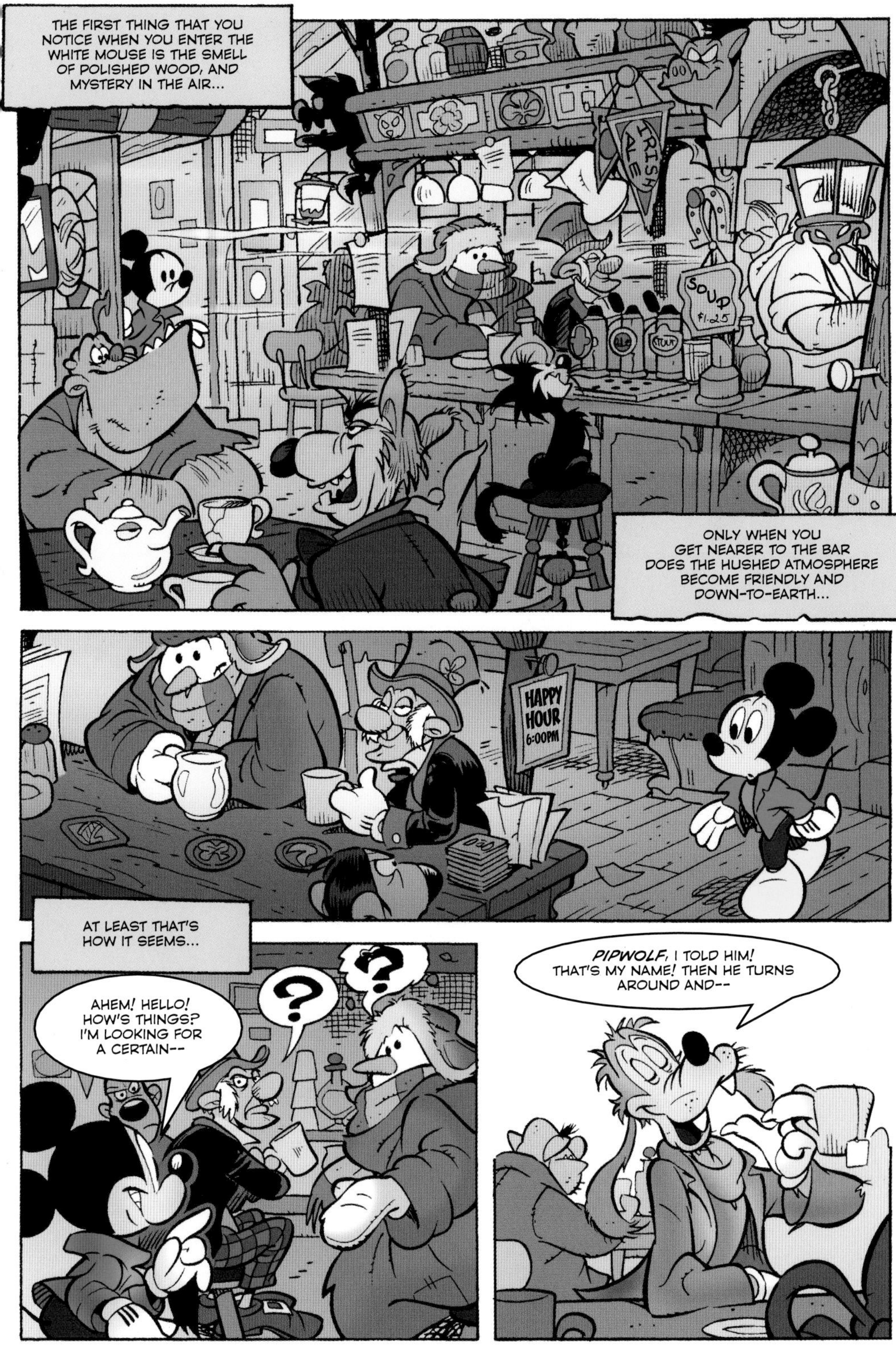
THE FIRST THING THAT YOU NOTICE WHEN YOU ENTER THE WHITE MOUSE IS THE SMELL OF POLISHED WOOD, AND MYSTERY IN THE AIR...
IRISH ALE
SOUP $1.25
ALE
STOUT
ONLY WHEN YOU GET NEARER TO THE BAR DOES THE HUSHED ATMOSPHERE BECOME FRIENDLY AND DOWN-TO-EARTH...
HAPPY HOUR 6:00PM
AT LEAST THAT'S HOW IT SEEMS...
AHEM! HELLO! HOW'S THINGS? I'M LOOKING FOR A CERTAIN--
?
?
PIPWOLF, I TOLD HIM! THAT'S MY NAME! THEN HE TURNS AROUND AND--

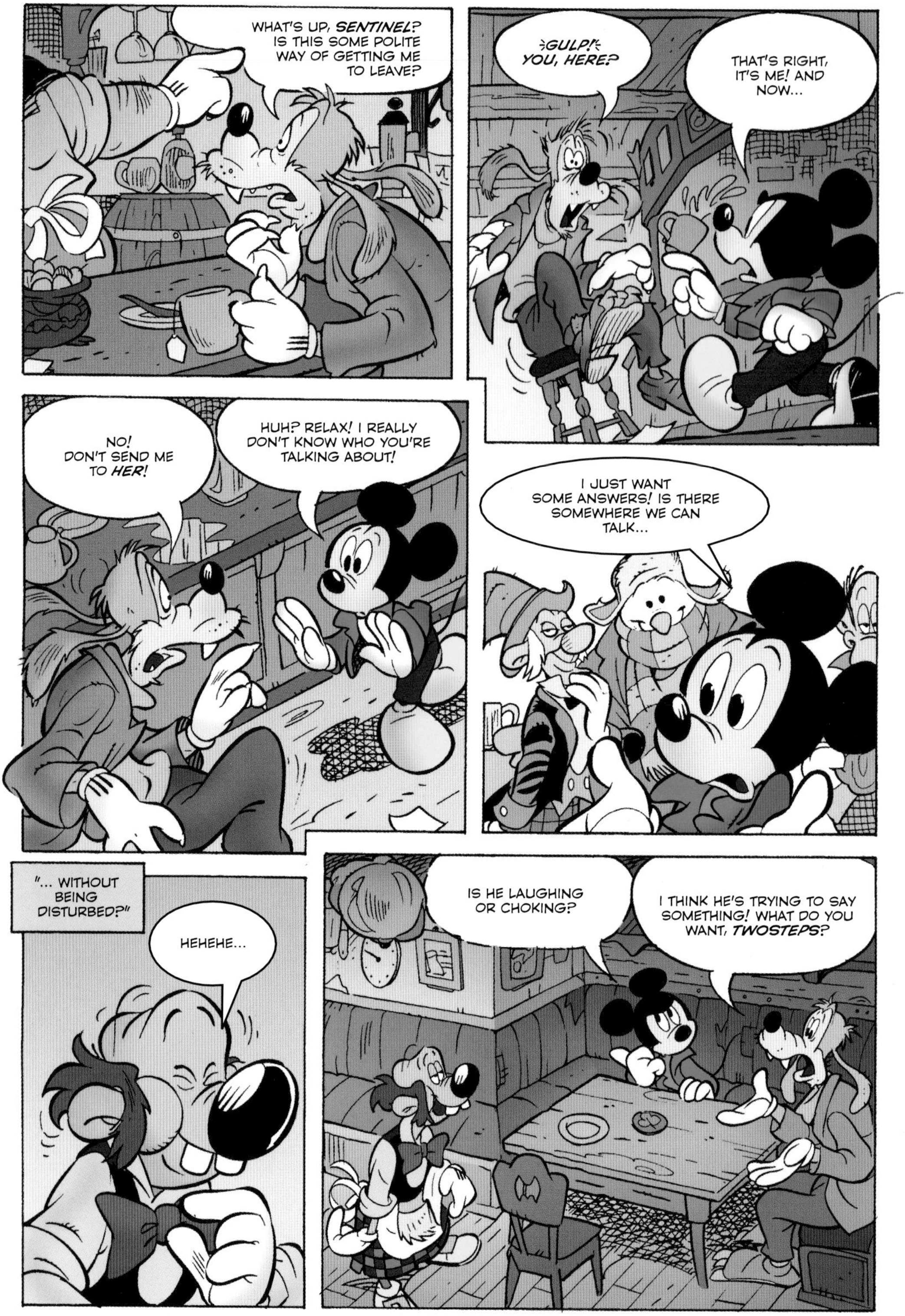
WHAT'S UP, SENTINEL? IS THIS SOME POLITE WAY OF GETTING ME TO LEAVE?
¡GULP!¡ YOU, HERE?
THAT'S RIGHT, IT'S ME! AND NOW...
NO! DON'T SEND ME TO HER!
HUH? RELAX! I REALLY DON'T KNOW WHO YOU'RE TALKING ABOUT!
I JUST WANT SOME ANSWERS! IS THERE SOMEWHERE WE CAN TALK...
"... WITHOUT BEING DISTURBED?"
HEHEHE...
IS HE LAUGHING OR CHOKING?
I THINK HE'S TRYING TO SAY SOMETHING! WHAT DO YOU WANT, TWOSTEPS?

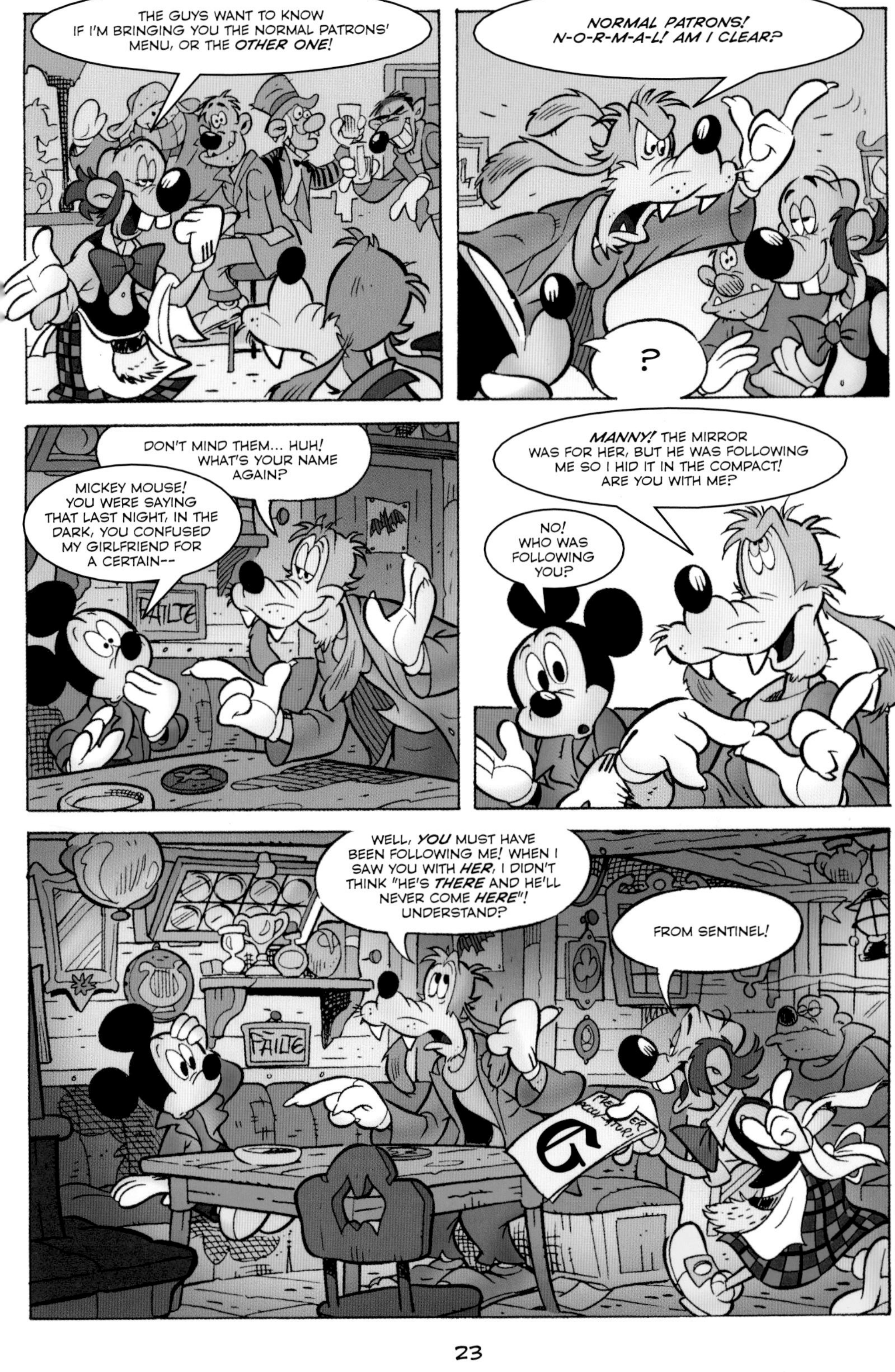
THE GUYS WANT TO KNOW IF I'M BRINGING YOU THE NORMAL PATRONS' MENU, OR THE *OTHER ONE!*
NORMAL PATRONS! N-O-R-M-A-L! AM I CLEAR?
?
DON'T MIND THEM... HUH! WHAT'S YOUR NAME AGAIN?
MICKEY MOUSE! YOU WERE SAYING THAT LAST NIGHT, IN THE DARK, YOU CONFUSED MY GIRLFRIEND FOR A CERTAIN--
FAILTE
MANNY! THE MIRROR WAS FOR HER, BUT HE WAS FOLLOWING ME SO I HID IT IN THE COMPACT! ARE YOU WITH ME?
NO! WHO WAS FOLLOWING YOU?
WELL, *YOU* MUST HAVE BEEN FOLLOWING ME! WHEN I SAW YOU WITH *HER*, I DIDN'T THINK "HE'S *THERE* AND HE'LL NEVER COME *HERE*"! UNDERSTAND?
FROM SENTINEL!
FAILTE

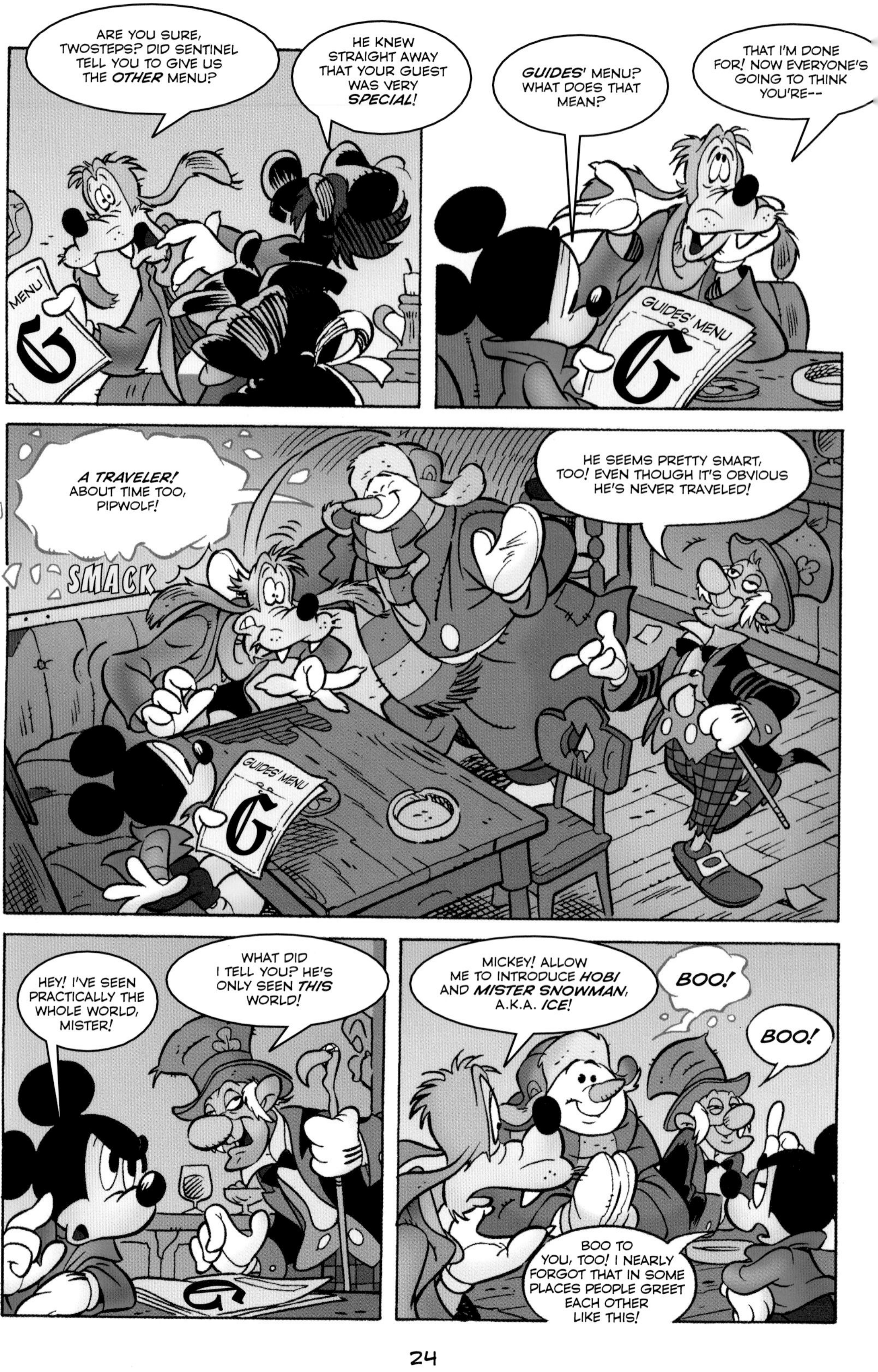
ARE YOU SURE, TWOSTEPS? DID SENTINEL TELL YOU TO GIVE US THE *OTHER* MENU?
HE KNEW STRAIGHT AWAY THAT YOUR GUEST WAS VERY *SPECIAL*!
MENU
G
GUIDES' MENU? WHAT DOES THAT MEAN?
THAT I'M DONE FOR! NOW EVERYONE'S GOING TO THINK YOU'RE--
GUIDES' MENU
G
A TRAVELER! ABOUT TIME TOO, PIPWOLF!
SMACK
HE SEEMS PRETTY SMART, TOO! EVEN THOUGH IT'S OBVIOUS HE'S NEVER TRAVELED!
GUIDES' MENU
G
HEY! I'VE SEEN PRACTICALLY THE WHOLE WORLD, MISTER!
WHAT DID I TELL YOU? HE'S ONLY SEEN *THIS* WORLD!
MICKEY! ALLOW ME TO INTRODUCE *HOBI* AND *MISTER SNOWMAN*, A.K.A. *ICE*!
BOO!
BOO!
BOO TO YOU, TOO! I NEARLY FORGOT THAT IN SOME PLACES PEOPLE GREET EACH OTHER LIKE THIS!

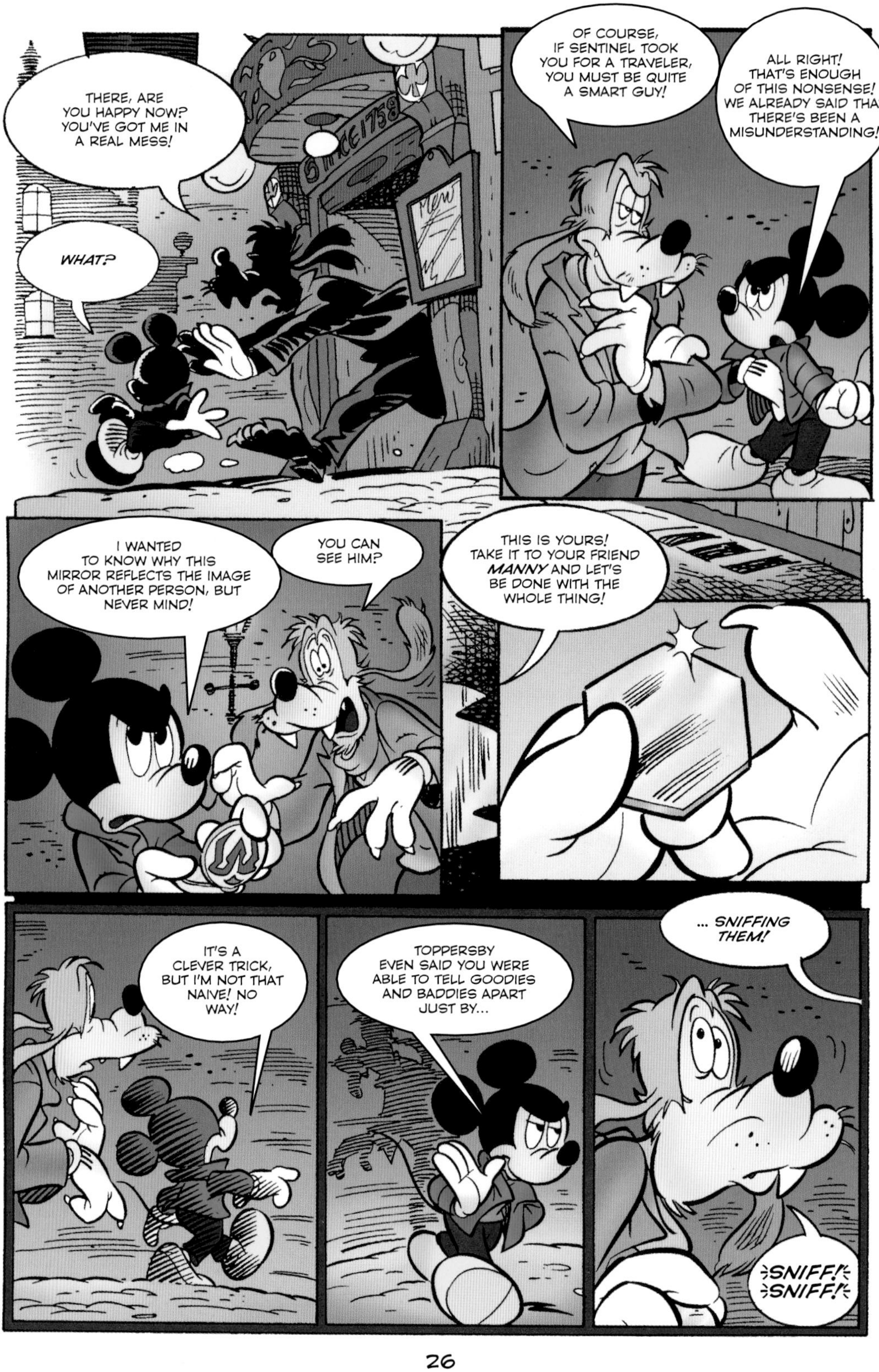
THERE, ARE YOU HAPPY NOW? YOU'VE GOT ME IN A REAL MESS!
WHAT?
SINCE 1758
OF COURSE, IF SENTINEL TOOK YOU FOR A TRAVELER, YOU MUST BE QUITE A SMART GUY!
ALL RIGHT! THAT'S ENOUGH OF THIS NONSENSE! WE ALREADY SAID THAT THERE'S BEEN A MISUNDERSTANDING!
I WANTED TO KNOW WHY THIS MIRROR REFLECTS THE IMAGE OF ANOTHER PERSON, BUT NEVER MIND!
YOU CAN SEE HIM?
THIS IS YOURS! TAKE IT TO YOUR FRIEND *MANNY* AND LET'S BE DONE WITH THE WHOLE THING!
IT'S A CLEVER TRICK, BUT I'M NOT THAT NAIVE! NO WAY!
TOPPERSBY EVEN SAID YOU WERE ABLE TO TELL GOODIES AND BADDIES APART JUST BY...
... SNIFFING THEM!
SNIFF! SNIFF!

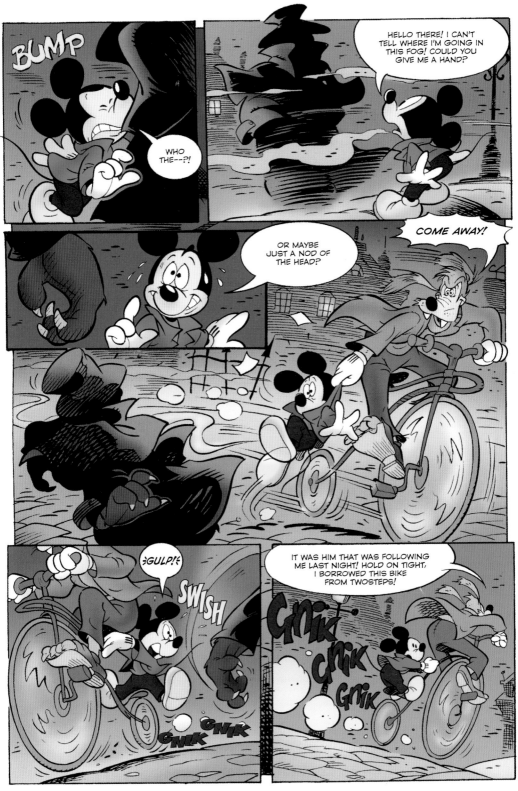

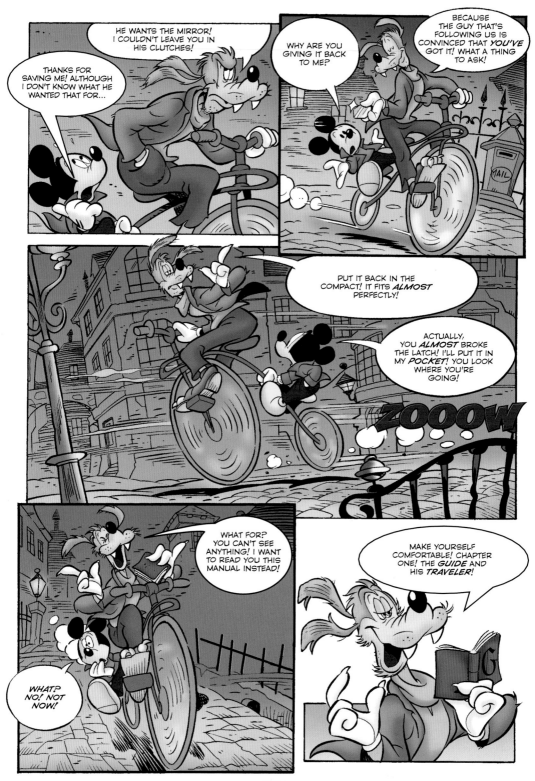

28

29

31

35

BUT I GAVE IT THAT NAME SO THAT TRAVELERS WOULD LEARN THAT WE DO THINGS VERY DIFFERENTLY HERE!

FOR THEM IT'S AN ADVENTURE, BUT FOR US IT'S CHAOS! NO RULES! NO CERTAINTY!

IT'S MY JOB TO ENFORCE THE LAW AROUND HERE! ESPECIALLY WHEN IT COMES TO *GUIDES!*

SO THAT'S WHY PIPWOLF AVOIDS YOU! HE CALLS HIMSELF A FREE SPIRIT!

ACTUALLY, HE'S AFRAID OF HAVING TO DO THE *OFFICIAL EXAM!* HE'S AN UNLICENSED GUIDE!

HE'S NOT A BAD GUY, BUT IT'S CLEAR FROM THIS POSTER THAT HE HAS AN AVERSION TO RULES!

WELL ANYHOW, HE WANTED TO GIVE YOU AN OBJECT SENT FROM TOPPERSBY!

AH *HIM!* HE WAS A GREAT GUIDE UNTIL HE *RETIRED!*

NOW I UNDERSTAND! HE KNEW THAT HE'D BE SAFE IN THIS WORLD! IT'S ABOUT--

41

42

CELANTUS! TOPPERSBY MENTIONED YOUR NAME BEFORE HE SENT ME AWAY!

I WAS HIS *CUSTOMER!* HE WAS SUPPOSED TO FIND THAT MIRROR FOR ME!

I'D BEEN LOOKING FOR IT FOR CENTURIES, BUT TOPPERSBY SUCCEEDED WHERE ALL THE OTHER ANTIQUE DEALERS HAD FAILED!

"UNFORTUNATELY, AFTER GIVING ME THE GOOD NEWS, HE MUST HAVE UNDERSTOOD THE TRUE NATURE OF THE OBJECT!"

"SO HE ENTRUSTED IT TO HIS *GOPHER*, BUT I WAS THERE WHEN HE GAVE IT TO HIM!"

"WHEN I LOST TRACK OF PIPWOLF I WENT BACK TO THE SHOP AND I SAW YOU!"

THE OLD MAN TRIED TO THROW ME OFF THE SCENT, BUT I FOUND YOU AGAIN AND FOLLOWED YOU INTO THIS *WONDERFUL* WORLD!

THE SHOP OF ERRORS
hp TOPPERSBY

ANTIQUES

OPEN

CLOSE

43

44

48

WATCH OUT FOR PAPERCUTZ™

Welcome to the spooky second DISNEY GRAPHIC NOVELS graphic novel—that's not a typo, the secret real name of this series is DISNEY GRAPHIC NOVELS, but for various crazy reasons we're not actually calling it that on the cover. Instead it seems easier to simply call this the very first DISNEY X-MICKEY graphic novel.

Why X-MICKEY? Good question! Let's just say, when this story first appeared in Italy, on April 30, 1998, there was a TV series that explored the paranormal that was very popular, and there's been a long history of using the letter X to denote the unknown and the mysterious, thus X-MICKEY was born. X-MICKEY is a series that features the one and only Mickey Mouse exploring all sorts of strange and spooky stuff. So, how exciting is that?

But even more meaningful to me—oops, I forgot to introduce myself. I'm Jim Salicrup, the Editor-in-Chief of Papercutz (and a one-time guest on the Mickey Mouse Club TV show), the comics company dedicated to publishing great graphic novels for all ages. So, as I was saying, what's even more meaningful to me is that Papercutz is at long last publishing an honest-to-gawrsh series starring Mickey Mouse. Just as Superman is the very first, and perhaps most important, comicbook superhero ever, Mickey Mouse is one of the earliest, and one of the most important cartoon characters ever. As Walt Disney himself would often remind his co-workers, as the Disney company kept growing more and more successful, "I hope we never lose sight of one thing, that it was all started by a mouse."

And it's great to see that Mickey Mouse is roaring back into American comics, in all sorts of forms. In fact, several great comics publishers are all presenting great examples of Mickey's colorful comics career. WALT DISNEY'S MICKEY MOUSE, a handsome deluxe hardcover series, that collects Floyd Gottfredson Mickey Mouse comics strips, which is published by our friends at Fantagraphics, while IDW has recently re-launched the long-running WALT DISNEY'S MICKEY MOUSE comicbook, featuring exciting Mickey Mouse adventures created by writers and artists from around the world. Not only will Papercutz be publishing X-MICKEY, we'll be featuring the fun adventures of Minnie Mouse and Daisy Duck in a series of graphic novels entitled DISNEY MINNIE AND DAISY! Plus we'll also be presenting another graphic novel series called DISNEY GREAT PARODIES that will recast the greatest works of literature (or shout we say liteRATure?) with classic Disney characters. We can't wait to publish Mickey's Inferno—the one that started the GREAT PARODIES series.

We hope you enjoyed this premiere installment of X-MICKEY, written by Bruno Enna and drawn by Alessandro Perina, and enjoy all the Disney Comics now available at bookstores and comic shops. Not to mention the following bonus pages from DISNEY FAIRIES #18 "Tinker Bell and her Magical Friends."

And remember... The Goof is out there!

Thanks, Jim

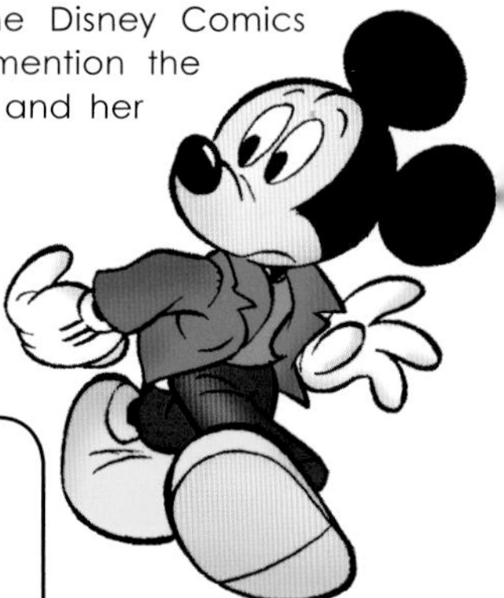

STAY IN TOUCH!

EMAIL:	salicrup@papercutz.com
WEB:	papercutz.com
TWITTER:	@papercutzgn
FACEBOOK:	PAPERCUTZGRAPHICNOVELS
FAN MAIL:	Papercutz, 160 Broadway, Suite 700, East Wing, New York, NY 10038

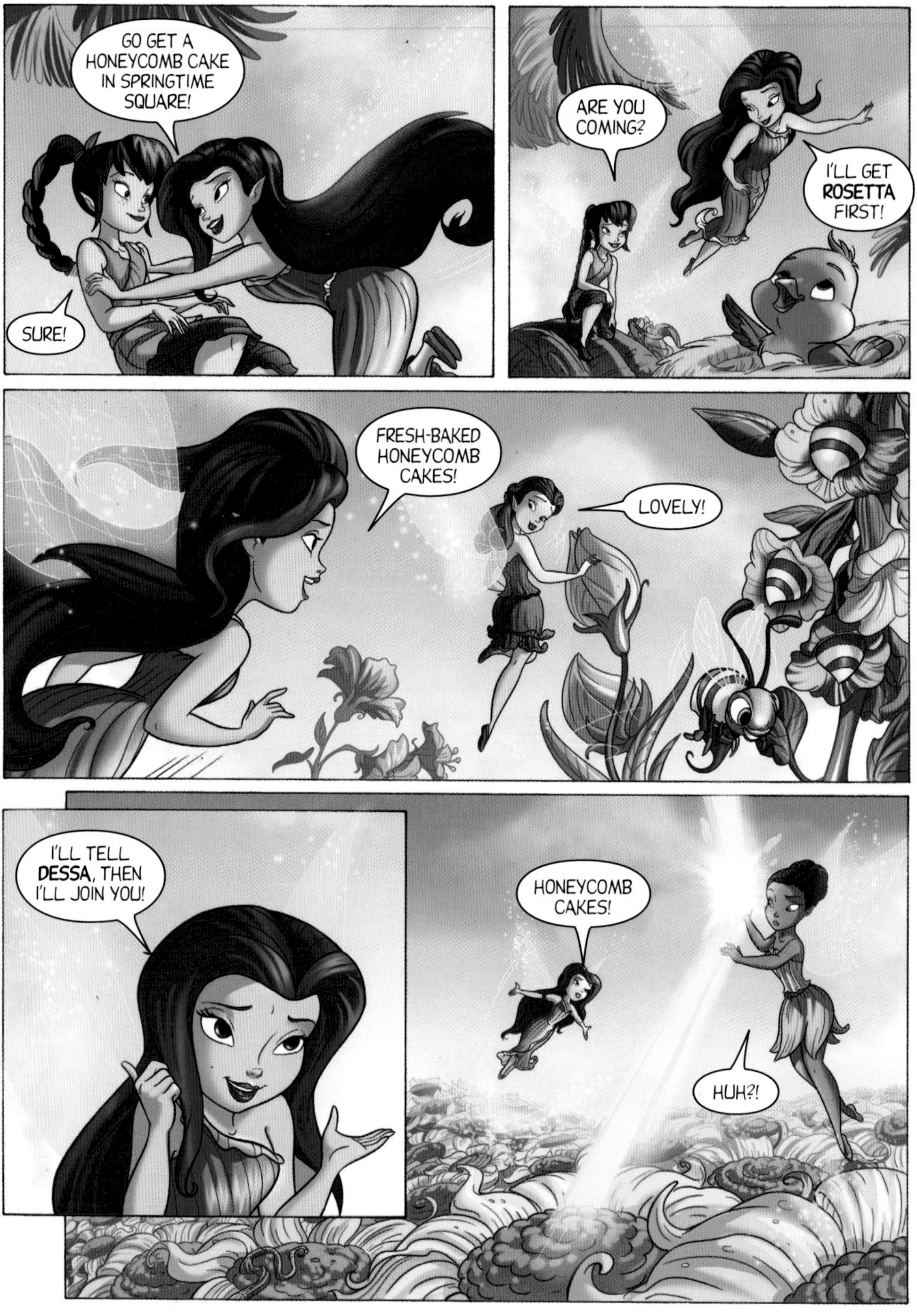
GO GET A HONEYCOMB CAKE IN SPRINGTIME SQUARE!
SURE!
ARE YOU COMING?
I'LL GET **ROSETTA** FIRST!
FRESH-BAKED HONEYCOMB CAKES!
LOVELY!
I'LL TELL **DESSA**, THEN I'LL JOIN YOU!
HONEYCOMB CAKES!
HUH?!

THE END

Beautiful Ribbons

THE END

Hop, Hop!

Don't miss DISNEY FAIRIES #18 "Tinker Bell and her Magical Friends," on sale now.